Best of Enemies

Iain Parke

bad-press.co.uk

Also by Iain Parke

The Liquidator
Heavy Duty People
Heavy Duty Attitude
Heavy Duty Trouble
Operation Bourbon
The Lord of the Isles
DILLIGAF

ISBN: 978-0-9930261-5-7

iainparke@hotmail.com

For Eamon

1938–2017

This one really is for my father

We may therefore be sure that there is a plan, perhaps built up over several years, for destroying Great Britain.

Winston Churchill, 14 July 1940

Führer Directive 16

Preparations for the Invasion of England

As England, in spite of the hopelessness of her military position, has so far shown herself unwilling to come to any compromise, I have therefore decided to begin to prepare for, and if necessary carry out, an invasion of England. This operation is dictated by the necessity of eliminating Great Britain as a basis from which the war against Germany can be fought and, if necessary, the island will be occupied.

I therefore issue the following orders:

1   The landing operations must be a surprise crossing on a broad front extending approximately from Ramsgate to a point west of the Isle of Wight... I shall be responsible for the final decision. The preparations... must be concluded by the middle of August.

2   The following preparations must be undertaken to make a landing in England possible:

    a   The British Air Force must be eliminated to such an extent that it will be incapable of putting up any substantial opposition to the invading troops.

    b   The sea routes must be cleared of mines.

    c   Both flanks of the Straits of Dover, and the Western approaches to the Channel... must be so heavily mined as to be completely inaccessible.

    d   Heavy guns must dominate and protect the entire coastal front area.

    e   It is desirable that the English fleets both in the North Sea and in the Mediterranean should be pinned down... shortly before the crossing takes place... coastal waters should be attacked from the air and with torpedoes.

Adolf Hitler, 16 July 1940

Beginnings

Late October 2007

We had a dank grey day on the outskirts of Leatherhead for it, just after lunchtime, not that any of us had eaten.

I'd never carried a coffin before, none of us had. So as the mourners settled into their seats inside the crematorium, outside under the porch the undertakers gave us a quick and experienced briefing as they matched us up in height. I wasn't really taking much of it in, I realised, as we hoisted the weight onto our shoulders, but since they put me as a one of the back pair I guessed it didn't matter too much. All I had to do was follow the figure in front of me and not trip over his, or my, feet.

It was all about just getting through it.

They had reserved the front rows for family and having bowed to the coffin and turned away, I slotted into my allotted place beside Mum while Johnny Cash faded and the celebrant stepped up to welcome us all and set out our agenda for remembering and saying goodbye.

And then I was on my feet again. Stepping up to the lectern where my words were already laid out ready for me to read, I turned to face back into the room.

I looked up and out at a sea of faces, some familiar, many not, quickly registering who of the family were where in the hall.

His killers were out there, I thought. They and their paymasters. There would be someone here today, in the room, watching me even now. I was sure of it, but what could I do?

Then taking a breath, I began to speak the three pages of words I'd laboured over for the last week or so without glancing down.

The authorised version.

And tried to shut out of my mind the unauthorised one.

*

August 2007

In the early days they had used simple garage door remote controls.

But the Crusaders had soon worked that out from sweeping the radio waves for signals.

Then they had switched to mobile phones, but again the Crusaders had developed counter measures.

So, for security now they had gone back to basics, a command wire.

The Crusaders were wary of anything new, any pile of rubbish that hadn't been there the day before.

But under the roads were regular culverts connecting the drainage ditches on either side.

Far too many to search each time they went out, even if they were prepared to stop in the open to do so, and each with plenty of room for the oil drums.

And there was no spotting a command wire hidden in the dirt.

The sound rolled around the base a few minutes later. The rising pall of black oily smoke from out towards the airport road telling its own story as one of the gatehouse sentries sprinted to the command post to scramble the response team.

But even as the rapid reaction squads roared out a few minutes later, they did so with a sense of dread, knowing what they were likely to find at the scene. The lightly armoured snatch Land Rovers wouldn't have stood a chance.

Everybody knew that.

*

Late September 1962

The panel considered the young man sitting in front of them.

They had his file from his time in the RUC and they had his test scores; sixth nationally in the year's Civil Service exams, an impressive result. If he'd come from the right school and been to Oxbridge for a double first in classics, or perhaps at a stretch PPE, then he would have surely been a shoo-in for the fast track, and they'd probably then be thinking Cabinet Office.

But they had his file. Straight from school and into the police, and now looking to move over to this side of the water. So obviously not.

Married? Yes. Well that was good at least.

Children? One on the way, due May next year.

'So, what are your ambitions?' asked the ex-naval officer on the right of the panel.

'I'd like to do well, he told them, I want to make a success over here. I didn't have the opportunity to go to university and I'd like my children to have that chance...'

'My dear chap,' interrupted the Home Office representative in affable surprise, 'your sort's sons don't go to university you know...'

The ex-naval officer shot a look of pure venom along the bench, before his eyes flicked back to the now stony faced young man in front of them. As the tweedy duffer burbled on, completely oblivious to the impact he'd just had, the ex-naval officer gave the young man an almost but not quite imperceptible nod and made his own private notes on the application to follow up later.

*

A lifetime ago

Some left during the day, some left at night, but one by one over the last two weeks in November, the ships slipped their moorings, each setting out to sea on their own apparently unrelated missions, only to disappear under complete radio silence.

Not that their radios were silent. Indeed, each ship had deliberately left its assigned radio operator behind in port so that anyone monitoring the airwaves would hear normal levels of radio chatter and the distinctive keys of the individual wireless men.

Once out on the dark and wary winter ocean however, each ship set course to join its companions as the fleet began to assemble in the cold, remote, northern harbour. Meanwhile beneath decks, men worked furiously on fitting the special wooden fins and noses which had been developed through a frantic programme of testing and trials, knowing they had little time to complete the modifications required to the equipment to ensure there would be sufficient quantities on hand for their mission.

Eventually every vessel, from the huge battleships and carriers, to the tankers, screening cruisers, destroyers and outlier submarines, nosed its way safely into the anchorage to begin loading their supplies for the journey. Security on the surrounding desolate islands was extraordinarily tight as they did so. No one went in, no one went out. There was no shore leave, no radio messages, even no garbage overboard. Absolutely nothing could be left to chance that might endanger the secrecy of their mission.

Then at last they were ready, every nook and cranny stuffed full of the fuel and provisions that would enable the force to complete its task, assuming they received the final order to go. It was a call which would not be transmitted until they were already well en route to the target, a destination known at that stage only to a very small clique of senior officers across the fleet.

But for now, the instruction was to proceed, to set sail to reach their assigned jumping off point almost two weeks steaming away on a route designed to keep them far away from the normal shipping lanes and any chance detection. So, at dawn, while a bitter breeze billowed fog across the freezing waters, the armada weighed anchor, and led by their shepherding pilot boats, began to file slowly and menacingly out of the harbour.

They were on their way.

*

September 2007

The hotel was in the seedier backstreets just behind Paddington station. At the centre of a short terrace of tall Georgian high fronted townhouses that had seen better days. And better clients I guessed.

Ask for room six at reception the letter had said, and so I did.

'Ah, room six,' said the receptionist with a hint of a Polish lisp from her dingy cubbyhole. 'The gentleman left a message for you. He asked if you would wait for him in his room upstairs.'

This all felt very strange, I thought, as I walked up to the first floor. I almost hadn't come, but there was no denying it had piqued my curiosity. After all, it's not every day you get an unsigned letter in the post, at an address that isn't yours, inviting you to a meeting in a hotel room and demanding that you come alone and don't talk to anyone about it.

At least it didn't happen to me anyway.

And then to find that he, whoever *he* was, wasn't there, but I was to go up to the room alone. As I stood outside the door to number six, key card in hand, I wondered what on earth was going on? All sorts of half remembered film noir clichés ran through my mind. Was I being set up for something?

I swiped the card and pushed open the door.

Well there was no dead body as far as I could see. Which was a good start, I supposed. You could tell I didn't have high expectations.

As I looked around, the room was much as I had imagined it would be. A seedy, pokey slice divided out of what would originally have been a much larger high-ceilinged room, the cornicing cut off as it disappeared into the partitioning stud wall, while a corner had been chopped out of the space by more plasterboard walls to make a bathroom. Dull patterned wallpaper, heavy draping curtains to try and keep out the street noise and lights from behind the dirty windows, and a threadbare carpet that clashed with the patterned bedspread; not that you could see much of it in the sliver of space around the double bed.

There was an uncomfortable looking chair and a tiny desk in the corner. I opted for the bed and sat myself and my bag down to wait.

It didn't take long. The telephone rang within a few minutes.

I let it ring. But then I thought, 'What the hell?' It had to be for me. It had to be him. I picked it up.

'Hello?'

'Hello,' said a voice, 'You are alone, I take it?'

Chapter 1

Bodyguard of Lies[1]

The History of Operation Cassius – World War II's Greatest Secret[2]

By

Commander Sir Tom Belvoir DSO Royal Navy (Retired)

The personal award by the Emperor himself of an ornate katana, the ceremonial sword of a samurai, was quite simply the highest military honour that Imperial Japan could bestow. It was one they granted only three times during the whole of the war to members of their German allies. Two of the recipients were world famous; Reichsmarshall Herman Göring and Generalfeldmarshall Erwin Rommel.

And on 27th April 1942, a year and a half after the fall of Singapore, it was the turn of Kapitän zur See Bernhard Rogge to receive this signal honour. What had led this relatively unknown commander of a converted merchantman turned highly successful surface raider *Atlantis* to be honoured by the Chrysanthemum

---

[1] Due to an injunction obtained by Her Majesty's Government in 2011 on grounds of national security and breaches of the Official Secrets Act, Commander Sir Tom Belvoir's memoir *Bodyguard of Lies* may not be published in the United Kingdom. All extracts used in this book are therefore taken from the original Australian edition.

[2] To quote the National Archives website:
The National Archives has records from the various military security and intelligence services as well as GCHQ, MI5 and (to a far lesser extent) MI6. Historically, intelligence has been gathered by individual branches of the military as well as centrally by the government security and intelligence agencies.
Because of the sensitive nature of intelligence work, many files have been destroyed and others are retained in order to protect the identities of those involved in gathering intelligence.
This is particularly true of files relating to the Special Operations Executive (during the Second World War) and MI5 and MI6.
It is a matter of record that no British files relating to Operation Cassius have yet been declassified.

Throne were his actions in the Indian Ocean on the morning of 11th November 1940, for which he had already been awarded the Oak Leaves to his Knight's Cross.

*

QQQ, code for I am being attacked by an enemy raider. The Norwegian wireless operator tapped furiously knowing he had little time. QQQ, QQQ, QQQ.

The British Blue Funnel Line ship *SS Automedon* was one of those solid and reliable merchantmen which were the backbone of trade across our far-flung empire of those days. Already approaching twenty years old at the outbreak of war, if all went well there had been no reason why she wouldn't have been expected to serve another twenty, plying her trade between home ports and our possessions on the other side of the world.

But of course, war had made differences to the *Automedon*. Now her appearance was different, a drab coat of Admiralty grey and a World War I vintage 4-inch gun mounted aft to be manned by one experienced gunner and a handful of hastily trained deckhands. Her route was different, it now avoided the Mediterranean and took her down the West Coast of Africa to Freetown, on round the Cape to Durban, before she set out across the wide Indian Ocean as she headed for Singapore. And her cargo was different, a mixed supply of all the things needed for war, from crated up vehicles, aircraft, instruments and machinery, to uniforms, cigarettes, whisky and mail, along with a pair of newly-weds returning to Singapore.

But life on board hadn't changed very much from peacetime. So far, the trip had been uneventful, peaceful even. The weather had been fine all the way, the war seemed a long way off under the clear blue skies of day, and the familiar rhythms and routines of ship life as day followed day, gave a sense of security.

Until the evening of the 10th November, as they trailed their phosphorescent wake under the star-studded blackness heading towards the North West tip of Sumatra, when the radio operator picked up the Morse signal. QQQ, QQQ, QQQ.

It was partly an urgent call for help, and partly a warning, and the sender giving its location as somewhere 600 miles away from the *Automedon*'s current station was the *Ole Jacob*, a Norwegian oil tanker reporting an unknown ship coming after and then stopping them.

A little while later a message came through from the same transmitter, cancelling the QQQ message. Unbeknownst to the wireless operator on the *Automedon* and the officers now standing beside him in the cramped cabin, the *Ole Jacob* was already in the hands of a German prize crew whose chief had organised the cancelation message.

Worse still, they had no way of knowing that the original message, sent in such haste, had been incorrect. The *Ole Jacob* had in fact been boarded less than 200 miles away from the *Automedon*, less than a night's sailing for a fast raider.

*

June 2007

He put the file down on his desk and rubbed his eyes.

The irony of at least somebody having had some recognition for their part in the operation, even if it was a role they had no way of knowing they'd been given, still gave him some grim satisfaction even after all these years. Although he doubted anyone else would see the funny side, not that they would ever get the chance; he sighed as he closed the file and slipped the folder back into his desk.

Christ, he thought to himself with a flash of irritation, if not bitterness, as he locked the drawer shut, how many war memoirs must there be out there, lying forgotten in dusty attics and dark cupboards? Old men and women's memories consigned to faded ink and yellowing curling paper. The best and worst years of people's lives, times of intense emotion, now silent and entombed in obscurity.

Once again, he asked himself why he'd taken the time and trouble to write it. After all, if there were some things that were destined never to be revealed, then one thing he knew for sure was by God – this had to be one of them.

But then that was his nature and the way he'd been trained. It was a report. For any operation there was always a report. And for this operation, this was his.

Even if no one was ever going to read it.

He glanced down again at the two letters on his desk. One typed on letterhead with its familiar logo, the other handwritten in a familiar scrawl from long ago. His hand automatically went to put them both through the shredder, to join the bag of strips to be burnt later, when something stopped him and he considered it again. Well, he thought, it could wait. After all, he didn't have to make a decision now.

And it certainly wouldn't be some BBC researcher, no matter who he was! He smiled to himself as he slipped the letter back into a file of pending correspondence, and the keys into his pocket, before lifting himself stiffly out of the chair, while the sound of small children's voices drifted in from the garden in answer to their father's call.

*

As he stepped out into the hallway he heard the sound of Tim and Rosie, his great-grandchildren, being organised for the off at the end of the weekend and their father's leave. Toys were being checked as all present and correct, coats being gathered to go back in the car. Marshalling them and all their gear for the drive down to Plymouth sounded like a military operation these days, but then, that ought to suit his grandson and his wife down to a T.

'Right,' he heard John say as he reached the hall and looked out onto the drive where the estate car's boot was being shut with a thump. 'That's it, I think we're ready to leave you in peace.'

'Assuming you've got everything?' he asked.

'Well there's always something isn't there?' Suzy laughed. 'Now then, Tim, Rosie, it's time to say goodbye isn't it?' and he knelt down in the doorway for a flurry of hugs.

With the children in the car, seatbelts fastened, and last chances to go to the loo taken before the off, the adults embraced. Promises were made for Suzy to come back up in a month's time, unless he wanted to come down of course?'

But he knew it would be six months at least before he'd see John again. His unit was being deployed the following week for an operational tour to Basra as part of the Royal Marine's contribution to Operation Telic, hence his embarkation leave and this visit. Security duties and training Iraqi forces was the formal mission. Laying the groundwork for a post occupation Iraqi Training and Advisory Mission was the official description.

Continuing to fight a highly effective and deadly insurgency was the unofficial one.

An overt mission for public consumption, and a covert one. It was always the way wasn't it?

He waved the car off down the gravel drive and stood for a few moments after it had disappeared out of sight beyond the rhododendrons. He closed his eyes and felt the warmth of the summer sun on his skin, smelt the scent of the flowers in the air, heard the quiet buzz of a bee going about its business.

Then he turned, and shutting the door behind him, went back to his study to collect a few bits and pieces to take through to the kitchen. He liked to keep the place tidy. It was another of those long old established habits, never to leave anything lying around. A place for everything and everything in its place. It was one of those things the Services taught you.

Reaching up to turn off the light he glanced across to the line of family photographs on the mantelpiece and smiled.

It had been worth it. All of it.

*

Looking back now it can be difficult for people to remember, or if they weren't there at the time, to imagine, the situation we were facing in the autumn of 1940.

People remember Sealion and the threat of invasion but leaving that aside there was the very real threat that we might simply be starved into surrender by the U-boats of the German navy.

Even in those days we depended on importing food and critical supplies like oil to keep the country going, but by late 1940 our imports had already fallen by about twenty-five percent from a rate of sixty million tons to forty-five million tons a year.

Bluntly, we had lost the land war on the continent and now we were losing the sea war in the Atlantic. Following the fall of Norway and France, Dönitz could concentrate all his U-boats on the Atlantic and the effect was truly devastating. Once they were able to operate from bases on the French west coast rather than from the North Sea, their ease of access and the length of time they could spend on station in the shipping lanes went up dramatically, and so did our losses.

In July 1940 the U-boats had sunk thirty-eight ships, equivalent to about two hundred thousand tons of shipping. In September 1940 we lost fifty-nine merchant ships and in October 1940 we lost sixty-three more. That represented something like six hundred and fifty thousand tons of shipping gone in two months. But that wasn't the worst of it.

Thirty-two of those vessels went down in a period of only three days starting on the 18th October when a Wolfpack of nine U-boats attacked two convoys on their way over from Nova Scotia.

Operation Sealion or no Sealion, it was plain that we simply couldn't last at such a rate of losses. It was agreed by all concerned that something had to be done.

*

July 2007

'In World War II we were America's essential ally. Now we're America's poodle. How did we get from one to the other? That's the pitch,' she'd told me when she'd brought me on board a few months ago to support her development work.

The producer wasn't needing to sell the concept to me. I was just a researcher, I just needed a briefing. Tell me what you need me to find, and I'll go away and find it. That's my job.

And she was still selling it to me every time we spoke about it, even now as she came back with the news. But I didn't mind, I was used to it by now. To get something like this commissioned she'd have needed to have been rehearsing, refining, honing and delivering her elevator pitch for so long now, to so many editors and channel heads that it had become second nature.

'It's something that's of huge public interest, so our plan is a major series. A landmark documentary, a historical overview across four hour-length episodes taking the viewer right up to the Iraq war. We'll be looking to explain the decline of the special relationship, what it meant then, what it means now...'

'And how it got us into the current mess in Iraq?' I had nodded when we first spoke, seeing how what she was planning could get current affairs and history to both sign up to the sort of budget this would be looking at.

'Exactly. All that sort of thing,' she looked pleased that I got it. But really it was hard to miss.

'We're kicking off with Suez is the plan,' she'd told me.

At which I must have looked a little surprised.

'No really,' she'd insisted, 'It's the perfect place to start. It plays both backwards and forwards. Eden and Eisenhower were both high up and worked together as allies leading up to victory in the war. By '56 Eden is Prime Minister and Eisenhower is President. It's the height of the cold war, they're NATO allies, so if anything, you'd be expecting them to be able to cooperate together closely, yes?'

I had shrugged an agreement.

'Yet then along comes Suez, and Eisenhower just hangs Eden out to dry. It's a great jumping off point. It's got everything we need to make it relevant to today. The writing really was on the wall with this one.'

I could see what she meant.

And obviously so could the commissioning powers that be who'd just signed off on her budget.

*

Monday 21st October 1940

Men were gathered in knots around the edges of the room when, having shown my pass to the MPs on duty, I slipped in through the double doors just after eight in the morning. Discreet conversations were being conducted in hushed tones as we waited for everyone to arrive and the conference to kick off. A gentle fug of smoke was already perfuming the room.

Unsure of the form as it was my first day, I collected a cup of NAAFI tea from a table manned by a couple of WAACs and stood back into one of the window bays to observe the room as I waited for my new boss to arrive. I wasn't meaning to eavesdrop, but given the brief I'd been given by my old section chief on taking the secondment it was difficult not to, I did need to think about the job I'd presumably be going back to in due course, after all.

And it was particularly difficult, given the nature of what I realised I could just about overhear of the two men's conversation in the alcove next to where I had perched myself out of the way.

'Surrender?' my ears pricked up at the word.

'Seek terms is what I said. You heard yesterday's news about SC7 and HX79?'

'The convoys?'

'Yes. Over thirty now isn't it?'

'Thirty-two all told.' The unfolding U-boat disaster off Nova Scotia. It was all anyone was talking about in Whitehall's corridors over those first few days.

'Jesus.'

'Well then, you know as well as I do how serious it is.'

They weren't whispering, I noticed. That would have been too obvious, the sort of mistake an amateur would make which would have risked drawing too much attention to themselves. Instead the tone was the sort of discreet and calm Civil Service murmur. It was a style designed not to carry too far, or to unwelcome ears, and one which I'd noticed seemed to become a natural way of speaking the more senior the user became.

These men were experts at it. Only the fold of thick curtain between where I stood and their position, not huddled in the next bay as such, but definitely tête à tête, meant I was close enough to hear, but also out of sight.

'Of course.'

'Have you seen the thing we've just had in from Stephenson?'

'The McCollum paper?'

'No, but I've heard the gist.'

'What do you think?'

'It'll come.'

'But when? That's the point isn't it?'

'Well, not for a while I don't think. Our friends are losing patience and are starting to think about an oil and steel embargo as a way of forcing them to the table.'

'Will it work?'

I wasn't sure who they were talking about. Force who to the table? And who were our 'friends' in this instance? As discretely as I could, sliding forward a little, I let my gaze wander around the room as I raised my cup and took a sip, my eyes gliding towards where they were stood, and then naturally away again towards the far end of the room. They were deep in conversation, but seemed wary, as I guess they might well be given what I'd just over heard.

The man in a tweed suit was the elder of the two, I'd have put him in his late fifties, with a military moustache and distinctly Brigade of Guards air despite his civilian suit. The other man was slightly younger, around fifty or so and wearing a Fleet Air Arm uniform.

'It may do. But once it's in place the analysts think they'll only have six months' worth of supplies. So that will leave them a choice won't it? To knuckle under to negotiations or try and grab what they want by force.'

'Which means?'

'Well they'll want oil, they'll want rubber, they'll want iron ore, they'll want coal...'

'All right, all right...'

'And it's obvious where they would go looking for them.'

'We're only just clinging on here as it is against the Germans. Can we really afford a threat in the Pacific as well?'

So, the Empire of Japan was the subject of discussion.

'But that's my point. We were facing a threat in the Far East anyway. That piece of paper doesn't change the problem one jot. You know as well as I do we're weak out there. You've heard about the memo to Brooke-Popham?'

'Just rumours.'

'Anyway, Hitler has postponed Operation Sealion so the immediate threat here is off.'

'Postponed it, yes. Cancelled it, no. It's a breathing space, nothing more.'

'But how long do you think?'

'Well as far as Sealion is concerned, for a cross-channel invasion they are going to want to wait until they can be reasonably sure of a long enough period of good weather. So my chaps think it wouldn't be before say, June of next year.'

'If we can hold out that long.'

'Well quite.'

'Do you really think that's what this meeting is about then? Surrender?'

'Coming to terms, I said.'

'*England is not our natural enemy*. Do you really believe that or that he could be trusted?'

'It would be the sensible choice.'

'Even if it were, he would never countenance it for a moment. You know how he feels about it.'

Up to that point, in some ways what I'd heard being discussed hadn't come as much of a surprise. This was a conference of extremely senior advisors and at that level of necessity there is a substantial degree of freedom of expression. After all HMG's policy makers have to have the best advice available, advice which takes account of, and objectively explores, all the options to help them decide what is in the nation's best interests.

So, for the sake of assessing the position on any issue, even and especially the life and death ones of wartime, nothing whatsoever could be off the table when it came to taking a view, whether they accorded with current policy or not.

But the next things I heard were of a different order altogether.

They really shocked me.

'Perhaps he'll have to, whatever he feels about it.'

'He's the Prime Minister for God's sake.'

'Prime ministers come, prime ministers go. Particularly when they're making mistakes.'

'What are you getting at?'

'Our duty is to the country, not to him.'

'He is the country.'

'Says who? Not the electorate. They never got a say, did they?'

'Maybe so. But we aren't the ones with the authority to do anything about it, that's parliament's prerogative.'

'What, with a national government and any general election postponed until all this is over one way or another? The reality is that we're in an elected dictatorship with no constitutional prospects of changing the prime minister.'

'Are you suggesting unconstitutional means should be used?'

'I'm not suggesting anything.'

Just then they were interrupted by noises from outside. I could hear the crunch of gravel, doors banging, the sound of voices and boots stamping to attention.

'Is that a car?'

'Yes. I'll just check.'

'And?'

'Yes. It's them.'

'Who's coming? Winston?'

'Yes. And the others.'

'Right.'

'Well I wonder what they want us for?'

'This should be interesting.'

'Shouldn't it just?'

Well quite, I thought to myself, as I hung back amongst the general gathering for action presaged by the noise of the arrivals on the drive outside. I waited until the two men had left their alcove and watched as they made their way down the room, splitting up to take their seats, before I made my own move towards my appointed place.

*

'Eden?' Dad asked that evening, as I told him we'd got the greenlight at last after all our prep and the series was definitely now on. There was no way I could afford to live in London, so it was lucky that Mum and Dad could put me up when I needed to work down here. As a researcher I wasn't usually tied to an office, it was a matter of going where the information took me on a project so even though it wasn't ideal, I'd got used to a life where I was away all week, and back up north to Salford at weekends where I'd bought a flat close to the new BBC hub.

'Anthony Eden? During the war? Well he was Foreign Secretary, wasn't he?'

He'd poured out a cup of hot water for me and handed it over with an Earl Grey tea bag for my swift dunk. Then he went back to warming the pot for what he regarded as a proper cup of real tea.

'Any chances of you finding a scoop?'

I laughed, 'Out of fifty, sixty, and seventy-year-old papers? I don't think so.'

'Well you never know.'

'I mean it's all ancient history now. There can't really be anything much that we don't already know, can there?'

'Still it's the war,' he mused, 'People are still interested. Otherwise why are they paying you to look?'

'True. Here's to an ongoing fascination with the era!' I said, raising my mug as he pulled out a chair opposite me and sat down with his cup and a couple of Rich Tea biscuits.

'Mind you, I doubt that anything you'd find would surprise me that much about Eden.'

'Why not?' I asked.

'Well you'd have to say he had form, don't you?'

'Oh, Suez you mean?'

'Absolutely. Faking a pretext for war and selling the invasion of a middle-eastern country to the public under false pretences.'

'Well thank God no one else would ever think of making that sort of mistake again,' I joked.

'Well quite,' he agreed, 'Amazing isn't it? Nothing much changes does it?'

'No, I guess not.'

That was the thing about Eden, the producer had said when I'd queried whether he was really a strong enough hook to hang the start of our series on.

'He used to be the fresh hope. At thirty-eight our youngest ever Foreign Secretary, the idealist, the man who resigned on principle over Munich,' she'd told me. 'And yet what's the only thing he's remembered for these days? A disastrous failed adventure in the middle-east.'

At the time I'd thought she'd been laying it on a bit thick. But now I had to admit from a focus group of one, she had been right.

'Where are you tomorrow? Here or up in town?'

'Neither. I'm off out Oxford way somewhere.'

'Oxford? What for?'

'It's my first interview.'

'Oh yes, of course.'

*

Dad was partly right as well. Scoop no. Opportunity yes. I was excited and very conscious that after the last half dozen years at the Beeb, this could be my big break.

Your career at somewhere like the BBC is all about building the right track record, your CV of credits on successful projects ticking up on IMDb, and by making the right contacts, preferably ones who are on the way up and whose coat tails you can latch onto.

The producer was definitely one of those people who was going places, a rising star. You could see she was being groomed for bigger things and this was her planned breakout primetime series, her first major project designed to enable her to show what she could do, make her mark.

A lot of big players had a lot of expectations riding on this series. And success would roll downhill by association.

Where to start is always one of your first questions as a researcher, but for a project like this the producer has always had to do some digging for themselves which you can take advantage of.

'I've fixed you up with an interview,' she'd told me. 'Sir Tom Belvoir. He's military, ex naval intelligence, he worked with Eden for years during the war, and afterwards was into the Suez debacle up to his neck. Must be ninety if he's a day but still has all his marbles I'm told. He's never talked before but we fired him an invite and surprise, surprise, he's said yes, so I need you to head over to see him. In fact, make him top of your list before he changes his mind.'

I nodded as I scribbled down the details she was giving me.

'Oh, and I've got you a research pass for Curzon Street,' she added.

It took me a moment to work out what that meant. But then I got it.

Curzon Street. One of the Secret Intelligence Service's old homes before they built themselves their James Bond green glass lair on the South Bank, and nowadays their archive reading room.

'I'm going to look at the Service's files?'

'Yes, it's where it started,' she'd confirmed.

Dad was just going to love this, I'd thought.

*

And what needed to be done in the first instance was all we could do, to attack the U-boats at source in their bases. Which as I knew only too well from personal experience, was a task for Bomber Command with its woefully inadequate equipment.

Charlie had been on his first bombing raid. On the 19th March he'd climbed into his Hampden bomber and taken off from somewhere in England, in fact RAF Hemswell in Lincolnshire, for a night time raid on the dock facilities, seaplane hangars and slipways of the port of Hörnum, in Sylt, Germany.

He had always loved flying Hampdens he'd told me. The narrow aircraft was more like a fighter in some ways, only three feet wide and nicknamed the flying tadpole. Once you were strapped in, you were in, with nowhere to go until you were back on the tarmac. But for its time it was fast and manoeuvrable, popular with pilots so long as the mission wasn't too long.

But as a fighting aircraft it had its limitations. The defensive armaments were woefully inadequate, while the pilot had to not only fly the aircraft but also had the bomb release catches to deal with on his run into the target.

*

Of course, once I'd printed a map off of where the house was and got out the road map to work out how to get there I realised that while it was in Oxfordshire, it was actually nowhere near Oxford. It was easy enough to find, with the map propped open on my knee as I drove. I've got a sat nav facility on my mobile but I've never been arsed to set it up and of course the only times I actually want it are when I'm running late or lost or usually both, and by then I don't have time to even think about trying to make it work.

So I was about ten minutes behind schedule as I drew up to a pleasant looking house of honey coloured Cotswold stone, right on the edge of a tiny village, a hamlet really, called Spelsbury, which was in rolling countryside close to Chipping Norton. Set on a corner plot behind neatly clipped hedges, the house fronted onto the road across a green well-tended garden. Just shy of the corner was a turning, a lane running past the back of the house and the neighbouring farm's barns on the other side. As instructed, after a few yards I turned into a gravelled driveway and pulled up, leaving my ratty P reg Toyota next to a relatively new BMW and a slightly older but brightly polished Volvo estate.

As a researcher, I've interviewed hundreds, perhaps even thousands of people in my time. My field has always been politics and history so I've spoken to the great and the good, as well as the not so great and the fairly bad. Even so, as I pushed open the garden gate and crunched down the gravel path towards the conservatory that ran along the back of the house, I was excited today about what I was going to do. After all, this was my first proper interview for what was looking like a major series that could get its makers noticed. And where better to start than with Commander Sir Tom Belvoir, DSO Royal Navy (Retired)?

Having read up on him in the afternoon after my meeting with the producer, I had honestly been surprised that he had agreed to see me. She was right, I couldn't afford to miss the chance to make the most of what was probably a once in a lifetime opportunity.

*

I saw a porch off to one side of the conservatory, so I stood at the door and rang the bell. There was a noise inside and then the sound of footsteps coming to the door before it was pulled open by a young slim woman, neatly and conservatively dressed.

'Hello. Can I help you?' she asked brightly.

'Hello there, I hope so, yes,' I said, proffering one of my Beeb business cards, 'I have an appointment with Sir Tom.'

'Oh, right then, yes he's expecting you. Well you'd better come inside,' she said, opening the door wider to let me in and holding out her hand in greeting, 'I'm Suzy Belvoir, his grandson's wife.'

'Thank you,' I said, stepping inside.

'Tom!' she shouted down the hallway as she closed the door. 'It's your BBC chap here to see you.

'This way,' she said, leading me into the house. 'He's in his study and don't worry, I was just visiting, I'll take you through and then I'll get on my way and leave you two to it.'

'Thank you very much,' I told her, 'but don't let me interrupt if you are talking.'

'No, it's fine, I was just here to deliver some bits and pieces and I'm done anyway,' she said, as she pushed open the door into a smallish room lit by a large window where the walls were completely lined with precisely filled bookshelves, the only decoration a row of family photographs in silver frames.

Sir Tom was a spry, wiry white-haired man sitting at a desk arranged in front of the window and a view out over the garden at the side of the house. He was aged ninety-two according to my files, but was looking bright as a button, with piercing clear blue eyes, what I assumed was a naval tie and sharp upper-class voice. He stood up as Suzy ushered me into the room and gave me a firm, if a bit frail, handshake, before indicating with a wave that I should pull up one of the other chairs.

'Right then, I'll be off,' Suzy said, after the introductions had been made and Sir Tom had sunk back down into his chair by the green leather topped desk which was bare, other than a pair of neatly piled in and out trays for correspondence, and an envelope lying open in the centre, with the letter and some photographs that it had obviously contained lying face down on top of it.

They hugged in parting. 'Can I get you anything before I go?'

'No, no thank you, Suzy. I'm sure we'll manage. And thank you for bringing these over,' the old man added, tapping the envelope as she turned to go.

'Of course. Think nothing of it. Well I hope it goes well and you get what you want,' she said to me by way of farewell, as she picked up her handbag from where it had been resting on a small sofa.

'Yes, thank you.'

'So,' Sir Tom said, settling back into his chair and considering me with a penetrating stare as the sound of her feet on the parquet departed down the hall towards the front door, 'what can I do for you, young man?'

'Well firstly thank you for making the time to see me,' I said, sinking into a very clubby armchair opposite his desk.

'Oh, don't worry about that,' he said, reaching for the glasses that hung on a chain round his neck before peering at the details on my card which Suzy had handed him. 'I'm retired.' He looked back up at me and smiled, 'So you see, I've got nothing but time these days.'

He placed the card on his desk where he could see it as though he might want to refer to it and fixed me with a stare. 'So young man, tell me, why do you want to talk to me?'

And so it began.

'I'm not sure how much my producer has told you,' I looked for guidance but all I got was that quiet stare, 'but we're researching for a history programme and she came across your name in the files at Curzon Street…'

'The files?' he interrupted, seeming genuinely surprised, 'You are being allowed to look at Registry files? To film a documentary?'

'Oh yes. We've been cleared, obviously and only have restricted access…'

'Oh really? But even so, you've seen files with my name in them, have you?'

'Well yes, Sir Tom,' I said, 'It can hardly come as a shock now can it? After all you were in the Service throughout the war which is the period we're researching at this stage. You were right at the heart of some of the key decisions and committees of the time and so your name is going to crop up in relation to many of the things we'll be looking at.'

He still looked concerned, 'Well I'm not sure at my age that I really want to be in any sort of programme at all, you know. I've generally managed to avoid it this far after all.'

'I'm surprised at that, Sir Tom,' I said, in all sincerity, 'I would have thought that lots of people would have wanted to interview you over the years to ask what you knew?'

'Some have tried,' he conceded, 'but I put most of them off.'

Which was interesting in itself, I thought as I pulled my notebook out of my bag. So why had he decided to talk to us, I wondered? I'd have thought there wouldn't have been anything special about the producer's request, but I decided, this probably wasn't the time to ask that question in case he changed his mind.

'So what is it going to be about then?' he asked, 'this series of yours?'

'Well the overall subject is the special relationship in the post war world, but to give the context and a lead in we're starting at the outbreak of war and the areas of diplomacy, deception and intelligence,' I answered. 'I'm interested in how the three became intertwined, and what conflicts and contradictions that would have caused.'

'Really? And what are you going to call it?'

'I think that's still being workshopped,' I saw him wince, 'but the working title for this episode is *Perfidious Albion*.'

'That's a bit judgemental isn't it?'

'I hope not, but it has to be something that will interest people enough to watch it.'

'Well that's true enough, I suppose,' he smiled. 'So well then, what do you want from me?'

I was doing well, I thought. We had managed to secure an interview with the man who didn't do interviews, off the back of the producer's frankly speculative letter that I wouldn't have thought had a chance of working. But here I was, he was talking to me, and I hadn't been thrown out on my ear. Yet.

I hadn't been joking when I'd told him why we wanted to speak to him. From what I'd picked up already, the producer had been right on the money. If Eden was the thread that we were going to follow, then Sir Tom, or Royal Navy Lieutenant Tom Belvoir as he had been at the start of the war, ran consistently alongside it. He would only have been in his early twenties or so at the outbreak of war, yet as I was seeing from the files, just like Eden, he had served on a series of key committees that seemed to have been at the very heart of Britain's intelligence and diplomatic operations throughout the war.

He was there for anyone to see who cared to look, and yet he had never as far as my researches had been able to discover, given any interviews. But even so, here I was, and I knew I needed to make the most of the chance.

The thing with an interview, I'd learnt over the years, is to get them talking. About literally anything to start with if you have to, anything at all. Nothing happens without them talking. With it, everything is possible. You need to establish a flow and in time a habit, of communication, conversation and even eventually in some cases, of confession.

'Well,' I had thought careful about how to begin. 'One of the areas I'm looking at first is the period just after Dunkirk. The time when there was a serious and immediate threat of invasion. From what I understand, how we responded to that then and the sorts of deceptions we used to fool the Germans...'

You have to judge where to start, to ease them into it. So you try to pick on something they'll find easy and interesting to talk about, usually something non-threatening, nothing contentious. Safe and comfortable does it.

'Dirty tricks you mean?'

'If you like. That and camouflage. They seemed to be the starting point for all the deception operations that followed.'

'Well I suppose they were...'

*

I had heard him speak before. Of course I had, the whole country had hung off his words on the radio that past summer as the Battle of Britain had raged above us in those clear skies. But it was something else to be addressed directly by him in the room as he spoke to us without notes.

Gentlemen.

Good morning and thank you for coming. I won't take long to say what I have to say and then I shall leave you to it.

As you all know, through the courage and sacrifice of our brave airmen, we have defeated the Nazi menace that is drawn up against us across the channel.

For now.

But great though this victory has been, we must be realistic. What we have won is time, and not the war. Winter is now approaching and with it the weather will deteriorate. The Germans, having had a bloody nose, will not risk a seaborne invasion in the coming months.

But does anyone here think that one defeat in the air will stop Hitler, he who has crushed the armies of Poland and France, who has occupied the continent from the Arctic Circle at the tip of Norway to the Mediterranean at the foot of the Pyrenees, from advancing against us as soon as he is ready?

Indeed, won't a defeat, the first he has ever tasted, merely infuriate him and make him even more determined?

We believe that he fears that in the event of invasion, the home fleet will sail and fall upon his barges and transports making a horrid slaughter. And indeed, in the event of invasion we would have very little option but to order such an attack.

But in this age of modern warfare, we would only do so with a heavy heart, as we know that we would be sending the fleet, upon which our security as a seafaring nation has always depended, into deadly danger.

It would be assaulted by the enemy's Luftwaffe *from its bases in Norway and across the Channel.*

It would face his submarines slipping from their pens and his battleships ready to sally forth into the North Sea.

And it would run the risk of minefields he would undoubtedly stretch in depth across the sea lanes to defend his flanks.

Gentlemen, we have to face the fact that if and when the invasion does come we may have no option but to cast the fate of our nation, and of our empire, on the single throw of the dice, sending our fleet into a battle that it may not survive or even succeed in, to protect our shores against the Hitlerite hordes.

And if he does land, what then?

It is true that if he comes next year we will have had time to be better prepared. But how much better prepared will we be, based on what we can produce on the home front available to us, set against the fruits that Germany will be reaping from a conquered continent?

Does any of us here today, really believe that we, this island nation, ranged alone against Hitler's might, sundered from the support of our Empire and the very lifeblood of supplies of the fuel and food we need to support our people and to continue to fight on by the sea and a siege of U-Boats, can survive and win?

But gentlemen, does any of us here really believe that for the sake of the world and for history, we cannot afford to do anything else but survive and win?

That then, gentlemen, is the situation that faces us. One of unbelievable threat to our very survival as a country and as an empire, one where we face seemingly impossible choices, and one where time is clearly against us.

But by God's help I believe that we shall win through and that impossible choices demand impossible solutions.

And so, I charge you gentlemen, with thinking the unthinkable and devising the impossible strategies with which we will face and overcome this situation.

History, gentlemen, and the fate of our country and empire, is in your hands. In my view this has been willed where what has been willed must be. And so you have my completely impossible blessing and good wishes for your work, whatever that might be.

And with that, his contribution to the meeting was over, and he was gone, disappearing from the room to be scooped up by his escort down to the waiting car and his next engagement.

We had our mandate, and with my new superior Eden in the chair, The Meeting began.

Chapter 2

History will be kind to me for I intend to write it.
Winston S Churchill (popular paraphrase/misquote)

Sir Tom spoke fairly freely for about an hour. He confirmed the degree to which he had been involved and the size and importance of some of the operations.

'Although of course, whatever we did, in the end it was the chaps on the ground who actually had to go in and do what needed to be done. All we could do at our end was our dandiest to see they had the best chance possible.'

Of course, they had all been very hush hush, and had continued to be so for years after the war in much the same way that the Ultra secret had been kept at Bletchley for years, only starting to emerge in the mid-seventies. But these days, since as he said, so much had already come into the public domain, he had received official clearance to talk to me about it now, to a degree.

The story he told me was familiar in its outline. The early days of desperate, sometimes even bizarre efforts at camouflage, of beach side pill boxes painted as ice cream huts to fool the enemy. Of frantic efforts in tactical deception, with dummy airfields laid out in fields to fool enemy bombing raids. Of fake fires set in the countryside at night to draw off the bombers. Of the decoys that worked and drew enemy fire.

Of the one that didn't, where the *Luftwaffe* dropped a wooden bomb on it.

*

It was 07:00 the next day when the lookout on the *Automedon*'s bridge spotted smoke on the far horizon. It was soon clear that it was on a converging course, although as there were plenty of Dutch merchantmen in these waters, the appearance of another ship wasn't of itself too much of a concern. Until about 08:20 that was, when the Captain was summoned back to the bridge by the second officer as the vessel was now only some two miles away and coming straight for them instead of giving way, as it should have done under the international rules for avoiding collisions at sea.

The Captain was about to order a warning signal to be flashed to the approaching ship when a puff of smoke appeared. Any doubt about what that meant was extinguished a few seconds later as they heard the bang, the whoosh of the shell and then the eruption of a fountain of water just off their bow. The *Automedon* was under attack and as they turned back to look at the assailant bearing down on them they saw it break out the ensign of the German Kriegsmarine, while the covers that disguised her armaments and allowed her to pose as a civilian vessel came down.

It was clear to everyone, even as Kapitän Rogge's *Atlantis* signalled the *Automedon* to stop and its radio operator got off its own distress call, that the British ship was vastly outgunned. Its single 4-inch would be no match for the six 5.9-inch main guns of the *Atlantis*, let alone its secondary armaments. Putting up a fight didn't seem to be an option.

Nevertheless, fight is what the *Automedon*'s Captain decided to do, as calling for full power, he swung his ship hard round to be stern on to the raider and ordered his sailors turned gunners to open fire.

They managed to get off three rounds.

By that time Kapitän Rogge had swung the *Atlantis* around in turn so he could bring all his guns to bear on the *Automedon* as she attempted to make her escape, and fired three full broadsides at what was almost point-blank range for those guns.

*

And then of the work in the Western desert, of digging a fake water pipeline to misdirect the Germans about where the attack at El Alamein would come. Of canvas 'tanks' mounted on trucks to be seen where we weren't going to attack, and tanks covered in canvas 'truck' bodies where we were.

'You know there's a lot of stuff about this in the public domain already?' he asked.

'Yes, there is,' I conceded, 'About Masterman, and the magician...'

'What the conjuror chap out in Egypt? Jasper Maskelyne?'

'Yes, and Clarke and so on, but of course most of them are dead now...'

'You heard about Clarke's arrest in Spain I suppose?' he asked, now thoroughly amused, 'in '41?'

'The time he was dressed as a woman?'

'That's the one. The ambassador had to bail him out. Damn nearly got himself sacked.'

I had read about it. You did have to wonder though. Here was a man who had known all of our most precious secrets, from the fact we could read the enemy's codes, to that we had turned all his agents in England and were feeding him back misinformation; a man who had been offered the job as head of London Coordinating Station to be in charge of all our deception operations; and then he manages to get himself arrested in Franco's Spain wearing high heels, stockings, a bra, and a floral dress; and it only nearly got him sacked?

What in God's name did you have to have done in the Service those days before someone started to wonder if you might be a security risk?

All good amusing stuff.

'Is that the sort of thing you want?'

I nodded, and then in the next breath I nearly blew it.

'And did this fit in with the PWE?' I asked innocently, ticking the next item off my list of notes.

'You're reading files on the PWE?' he asked sharply.

The Political Warfare Executive had been the secret body that had coordinated the creation of British propaganda during the war. Eden had been on the controlling committee from when it had been set up until it fell under Eisenhower after D-Day.

Again, as a link between the interaction of Eden and Eisenhower's wartime careers it had seemed a useful connection which was why I'd raised it.

'And why are you looking at that?' he asked.

'I'm not particularly,' I admitted, surprised that it seemed to be such a sensitive subject and frantically wondering how I could row back to safer ground. Just when it had been going so well.

'Propaganda's not my area of interest. I just came across it in some of the background reading around Eden. I was planning to get a couple of files out when I go in to Curzon Street, just to get a flavour of what it had been up to. Did you work with him long?' I asked, attempting to change the subject.

He let me off the hook, but his guard was now up, if it had ever been truly down. I guess the interviewee can learn a lot about what the interviewer does or doesn't know from the questions asked, or not asked. But that's just a risk of the game.

'Oh yes. From quite early on in the war.'

'And afterwards?'

'Well not immediately afterwards no, as Atlee got in and there was a Labour government. But then when the Conservatives returned to power in 1950 under Churchill again, Eden was back in the cabinet. By that time obviously I was higher up in the Service and I had some more dealings with him.

'But we're getting off the point a little here, aren't we? You were asking me about deception.'

'Yes, I was,' I said, picking up my pen again. 'Yes, that's great. But there was more than just tactical stuff too though wasn't there?

'The strategic level you mean? Yes. *The Man Who Never Was* and so on? That was the next level up.'

'Strategic?' I prompted, looking up from my scribbled notes. I had decided that I wouldn't ask to record what he had to say in the hope that this might help him to feel more comfortable about talking freely, but it meant I was going to have to rely on some fairly rusty shorthand which I would have to transcribe almost immediately while it was fresh in my mind. If I left it too long I knew I wouldn't be able to read my own scribbles.

Not that there was going to be much to read on that particular subject as it turned out. The habit of secrecy was too long established for my efforts to achieve much it seemed.

'I have to be careful about what I might disclose about strategic operations. As I say, the main facts are known and in the public domain these days, but I don't have clearance to talk to you about anything more concerning that level of material.'

I tried to draw him out but he politely and resolutely evaded the question, talking instead about his career, how he was part of a naval family and taking me over to point out the pictures on the mantelpiece.

His father had been the proud bearer of a fine full naval beard, decorated for service at Gallipoli, but then invalided out in late 1916 after being wounded in the dash to the South at Jutland. The call of a life on the ocean wave had obviously been way too strong however, and so once peace had broken out he immediately returned to the sea in the merchant marine, going on to captain freighters on the empire's sea routes to India and beyond between the wars.

Sir Tom himself had been a naval lieutenant at the outbreak of war and had stayed with the Service until his retirement.

His son Michael had retired, having served in the Falklands task force and risen to captain a frigate.

'And this,' he said, picking up the photograph on the end of the row of a tall young man in an immaculate uniform. 'This is John, Michael's son.'

'Royal Marines?' I asked.

'Yes,' he said, still looking at the photograph.

'You must be very proud.'

'I am.'

'And this is?' I asked picking up a black and white photograph of a young man, again in uniform.

'Ah that was my brother, Charlie.'

'But he's not navy?' I asked, studying the picture.

'No, that's right, he was the rebel of the family. He joined the RAF.'

'Is he still…'

'He was killed,' he said, matter of factly, as he repositioned the photograph in its place on the mantelpiece. 'On a raid during the war.'

*

There was a First World War recruiting poster I remembered having seen, presumably from before conscription. It showed a father sitting in a chair and looking somewhat uncomfortable as his children at his knee asked, *So what did you do in the Great War daddy?*

Well the truth was, when it came to my war, I sailed a desk, and sent other men to their deaths. And by the time it was ended you could lay many, many millions at my door and I'd find it difficult to argue with you.

*

The day before The Meeting, I'd made my way down to Portsmouth and the seaman's mission hospital. The old man was lying in the ward, recovering from his operation and by the signs of it, giving the doctors a hard time and the nurses a laugh.

We chatted for a while. The operation had been a success, as far as it went, but my father was a man who believed in being direct.

Hiding from things by not talking about them doesn't make them go away you know, he'd always said, and it was the same with the cancer that we both knew was eating him away from the inside now.

And he was still refreshingly blunt about his situation.

'Six months if I'm lucky,' was his response to my unasked question. 'I'll be up and out of here in a few days, but the quack says I'd be better off if I was somewhere warm.'

'Well I'll organise that cruise for you,' I told him. It was one of our old standing jokes.

'Yes, that would be lovely.'

There was a moment's silence.

'Anyway,' my father insisted, rushing in to cover the space that had opened up momentarily between us. 'Tell me all about this appointment of yours, well what you can anyway, I understand it's all a bit hush hush.' He sat back against the pillows with a slight grimace of discomfort, but he waved away my offer as I reached out to help him.

'After all, you can never tell who might be hiding under the bed, can you?'

In truth there was little I could say.

As a naval intelligence officer, I'd been acting as my service's liaison with Bletchley Park on the naval aspects of Ultra, the ongoing efforts and occasional early successes in cracking the

German Enigma coding system and so read all their operational coded radio traffic.

Now I was being seconded to Downing Street and the Cabinet Office.

'Well it's not very glamourous I'm afraid,' I told him, 'I'm sharing a broom cupboard of a room with my RAF counterpart.'

Just the mention of the RAF opened up another moment of mutual silence between us, but silence of a different character, a silence of raw fresh shared grief, and a concern from my father about my own obvious frustration.

'Now son, I know what you're thinking, but we both know it's not just about you staying safe. Your job needs doing, by someone who has the ability needed, just as much as sailing a destroyer, more so perhaps.'

My father could say it as often and as gruffly and as matter of factly as he liked, but that still didn't mean I was reconciled to it.

But it wasn't something I wanted us to fight about again, not when we had so little time, as all too soon I would have to get away to catch my train back up to town.

I knew I would need to be on my toes at my first meeting the following day as newly minted intelligence liaison for the Foreign Secretary and effective Deputy Prime Minister, the Right Honourable Robert Anthony Eden.

*

'So tell me, why are you so interested in Eden?' he asked later, as we were back in conversation. 'Of course, his links to the Intelligence Services went back well before the war, into the 1930s.'

Tom seemed to be reminiscing so I just let him talk.

'He was very interested in what intelligence could tell him, quite unlike say, Ramsay MacDonald. Did you know that when he was prime minister, he never saw an intelligence officer or spoke to one directly?' he asked. 'The only time he ever had contact with the Service he had the Cabinet Secretary stand in the doorway and relay questions and answers back and forth with an officer sat in an adjoining room.'

'Plausible deniability I think that's called, isn't it?' I said mischievously.

How much of this would ever make it to screen was doubtful, but for a researcher, particularly one who had an eye on the potential of a BBC Publications coffee table book to accompany the series, it was all brilliant stuff. The inside gossip, the stories that conveyed the culture, the way the people worked. This was all going to be crucial to getting the human side of the series and any story to work. To get the viewers, and in time if I played my cards right, readers, engaged with the characters we would be talking about as people; with hopes, fears and emotions, and not simply as cold chess pieces, actors in some pre-determined chain of events that led inexorably and inevitably from A to the B and then the C that we all know about and call history.

'I can think of several words for it, young man,' he responded. 'Mind you, the feeling was mutual. The Foreign Office was so worried about a Labour prime minister when he first came into office that they held back on showing him the decrypts GC&CS was achieving with Russian diplomatic traffic in case he handed it straight over to the Soviets!'

'GC&CS?'

'Government Cipher and Communications School. The code breakers, what later went on to be Bletchley Park and Ultra. The GCHQ of its day.'

'Eden was Foreign Secretary by then wasn't he? The 1930s I mean. Wasn't he against Chamberlain's policies and eventually resigned over Munich?'

'Well yes and no,' Sir Tom said reflectively, 'He'd been Minister for the League of Nations from 1934 and got bumped up to Foreign Secretary in 1935. As Foreign Secretary, he had access through the official channels to intelligence assessments of course.'

'Direct access?'

'Yes, summaries, papers, face to face briefings when necessary.

'At first you know, I think he probably wasn't against trying to find some accommodation with Germany. He'd fought in the trenches in World War I. He found out that he and Hitler had been on opposite sides in the same sector of the Ypres.

'At the start of the 1930s, whatever you thought of the Nazis, it was quite a respectable position to accept that Germany had some reasonable demands. The Treaty of Versailles was widely seen so by observers across the political spectrum as a punitive one which placed what was really quite intolerable interference in the domestic affairs of a sovereign state.

'So there was quite a degree of acceptance, if not actual sympathy, for some of Hitler's early actions, from many people in British politics, right up to and including the remilitarisation of the Rhineland. Its own backyard, people called it.'

'And that would have included Eden?' I asked.

'At that early stage I would say yes.'

'But by the mid-1930s, MI5 had agents in the Ausland, the Nazi party apparatus active amongst Germans who were resident here, the *Nazitern* Churchill called it. MI5 was the department first to formally warn the government in 1936 about the danger of German expansionist aggression, and that the policy of what went on to be known as appeasement, would not work.'

'Churchill was being fed information from within the Intelligence Services at this time as well wasn't he?' I asked.

'Yes, Churchill was seen as the leading figure amongst what was called the Old Guard. It's been an open secret now for a few years that throughout the late 1930s Desmond Morton had been providing him with details of what the Services knew about German rearmament and intentions. He had been Head of Section V at MI6 in the 1920s which dealt with counter bolshevism, which I guess is where he and Churchill would have first met up.

'You know,' he added as a digression, 'there's always been a lot of speculation that Morton was responsible for releasing the Zinoviev letter to the Daily Mail just before the 1924 election.'

I vaguely remembered that from a modern history class at school. A fake news story creating a scare about a Labour Government being used as a route for communist subversion, it had led to the defeat of Ramsay MacDonald's first Labour Government, and been used ever since as prima facie evidence of the secret Intelligence Service's willingness to interfere in domestic politics.

'But how would Morton have known the stuff he was passing on to Churchill?' I wanted to know.

'He was head of the Industrial Intelligence Centre of the Committee for

Imperial Defence throughout the 1930s and was responsible for gathering intelligence on foreign countries' armaments manufacturing capacities and plans.'

'And he was leaking this stuff to Churchill?' I wanted to confirm what he was saying, 'Who wasn't in the Government at the time?'

'That's right. A complete breach of security; and then Churchill made him his personal assistant during the war.'

'So, did Churchill and Eden work together as well at that time?' I asked, 'Before Churchill was appointed PM I mean?'

He stopped to consider that, leaning back in his chair and steepling his hands in front of him, 'Well, even after his resignation as Foreign Secretary, Eden and Churchill weren't necessarily natural allies. Eden was seen as the leading light of what the whips called The Glamour Boys. In fact, some thought that Eden would become the natural rallying point for disaffected members of the government rather than Churchill, but he wasn't as confrontational as Churchill.

'He abstained on the Munich vote rather than voting against the government for example and so he lost ground in the house. He had actually joined the army again as a major after the declaration of war.'

'But Churchill brought him back?'

'Yes. He appointed him Secretary of State for War and by the end of 1940 he was Foreign Secretary again, although of course when it came to dealing with the big men of the day Churchill liked to do a lot of the talking direct.'

'That must have been difficult for Eden mustn't it?' I observed.

'No, I don't think so. In reality everybody knew he was to all intents and purposes Churchill's deputy with a wide-ranging brief. Of course they didn't always get on.'

'Oh?'

'Oh yes. They disagreed on a lot of things.'

'Such as?' I asked.

'The special relationship for one thing. Churchill was very strong on it which was surprising as he was such an Empire loyalist, while Eden was quite critical of the US and the way they treated us as allies once they did come into the war.'

'And from the files I've seen, I'd assume you would have seen a fair bit of him during the war, Sir Tom?'

'Oh yes, in one way and another. In some respects from late 1940 I was very much his aide de camp, his go between with the Services.'

'Five or Six?'

'All of them.'

*

It was over in three minutes, by which time the upper decks of the *Automedon* had been reduced to smouldering wreckage under the impact of eleven direct hits. As a German boarding party under Kapitän Rogge's ADC Lieutenant Ulrich Mohr launched, they could see that almost all the superstructure had been shot away, the bridge and officers' accommodation demolished, and the boat deck and lifeboats smashed.

On board they found the dead and wounded everywhere. While he arranged for evacuation of the crew and passengers, Lieutenant Mohr began a swift search of the ship.

Kapitän Rogge's instructions were clear. As a raider, he needed the *Atlantis* to disappear back into the open ocean as quickly as possible. He knew that the *Automedon* had got out a distress call which would alert the allies to his presence and any ship in the area spotting *Atlantis* with the *Automedon* would immediately know what was going on, so the longer he remained by the stricken vessel, the more danger he put his overall mission in.

Nevertheless, vessels like the *Automedon* and the mail and charts they carried were potentially vital sources of intelligence which needed to be exploited to the full. So part of Mohr's mission on board in the time he had available was to turn safe cracker.

The mail room yielded fifteen bags of top secret correspondence intended for the British Far East Command. Labelled 'Safe hand – By British Master Only', these contained a wealth of material from decoding tables, fleet orders, gunnery instructions, details of minefields, naval intelligence briefings, through to maps, charts and notices to mariners, all of which were of value.

But it was in the captain's drawers in the chartroom, a floor below where he lay dead on the bridge that Lieutenant Mohr found the real prize.

Marked 'Highly Confidential, To Be Destroyed', as a security precaution, the green canvas bag had been equipped with brass eyelets so that if tossed overboard it would sink immediately. Lieutenant Mohr guessed the captain had kept it here so as to be able to reach it quickly and dispose of it over the side if the ship had ever been stopped, a plan foiled by the effects of the intense shelling in which the bridge had taken a direct hit almost immediately.

Inside was a single narrow envelope with instructions that it was 'To be opened personally' by Air Chief Marshall Robert Brooke-Popham, the Commander-in-Chief of the British Far East Command responsible for Singapore, Malaya, Burma and Hong Kong.

As Lieutenant Mohr quickly scanned the pages of the report it contained he was utterly astonished by what he was reading.

Why in God's name would Britain have risked sending such a critical document on a slow boat to Singapore? Lieutenant Mohr asked himself, as his boarding party returned to the *Atlantis* bearing supplies commandeered from the 550 cases of whisky and two and a half million Chesterfield cigarettes in the *Automedon*'s cargo, leaving her ready to be sunk by scuttling charges.

He simply couldn't understand what such a sensitive communication was doing being transported on an old merchantman like *Automedon*, and not guarded on a proper warship.

It just didn't make any sense.

*

By the end of the afternoon we'd got onto the Double Cross system of turning German agents.

He'd not been involved. 'It was operational, but as you'll know, we were very good at it. We used them to feed back a lot of misinformation throughout the war. Everything from the effect of Hitler's V-weapons to making the Germans believe Normandy was just a feint and the real invasion was coming elsewhere.'

'But really, you had to wonder about the codenames. Agent Zig Zag? That was my favourite. I mean what kind of code name is that for a double agent? They might as well have hung out a flag if the Germans had ever caught wind of them.'

'Well I suppose it had a lot to do with the atmosphere inside Five at the time,' he conceded. 'It was still quite clubby in the early days. So in some ways the codenames were often more of an in-joke than anything else. Agent Tricycle for instance was vital to the Normandy deception plan, but he was just called that because he liked three in a bed sex.'

'You're joking!'

He shook his head, 'I'm afraid not.'

'You're telling me the invasion plans could all have been put at risk if the Germans had linked a crude nick name with his kinky tastes?'

'Yes,' he nodded.

'Unless of course you were being sophisticated?'

'Oh yes?'

'A double bluff?'

'What? Name the really important things after seemingly obvious links so the Germans would dismiss the connections if they ever found them?' he laughed, 'My God you do think we were a devious bunch, don't you?'

'Well weren't you being paid to be?' I countered.

'I can't argue with that, I suppose.'

*

'Well thank you, Sir Tom,' I said, pulling my bag onto my knee. 'You've been very helpful and I'm very grateful to you for your time.'

'Not at all. I'm more than happy to help, and if there's anything more I can do, within reason, please let me know.

It was time to go and I didn't want to overstay my welcome. He insisted on walking me to the door.

'Thank you, Sir Tom. That was fascinating. *The Man Who Never Was...*' I asked as I followed him to the front door, 'Didn't I see a film about that?'

'Yes, *Operation Mincemeat* it was called.'

'Another classic codename?'

'Well quite,' he admitted.

'He was a man called Glyndwr Michael. Had died of TB, poor chap so his lungs were full of fluid. The team dressed his body up as a fictitious Major Martin, with everything from theatre tickets to a letter from his girlfriend in his pocket, and then they chained a courier's briefcase to his wrist with fake plans for an invasion of Greece. The navy floated his body and an upturned life raft off a submarine before dawn where it would wash up onto a beach in Spain. Of course, Franco's chaps fished him out and the Germans got to copy the papers before we had them back.

He slipped the latch and pulled open the front door for me.

'It was disinformation, a diversion from the real Operation Husky which was the invasion of Sicily. We got to be quite good at it really in the end.'

'A dodgy dossier eh?' I said, stretching out my hand to thank him, 'Zinoviev? Fake documents telling them we could invade in forty-five minutes or something? Nothing much changes does it?'

I could feel his mood suddenly turn as he showed me through the door.

'I wouldn't know anything about that, young man.'

Chapter 3

In England they are filled with curiosity and keep asking 'Why doesn't he come?' Be calm. Be calm. He's coming.

Adolf Hitler, 4 September 1940

Whenever I have thought about it, and the events that unfolded over the following week, which has been almost daily over the years since, I have always referred to it as just The Meeting, with capital letters.

As an introduction to my new job it was very much a case of in at the deep end.

I wasn't to know it at the time of course, but The Meeting was to end up lasting all day, a day which would change the course of history forever.

As intelligence aide de camp to Eden, my brief was to be his liaison with, and cut out from, all the Services; military, secret and the various private armies that seemed to proliferate throughout the war under Churchill's aegis, SOE, LRDG, SAS, SBS, Popski's private army.

That was the overt role. The day job as it were.

But my old commanding officer at naval intelligence was very clear about my covert role as well. As far as he was concerned, secondments were temporary and I still worked for his Service. I was to be his eyes and ears, and, *Was that clear Lieutenant?* To which the only available answer for a young officer with an eye on any future career at all in the navy, was a smart, *Yes Sir, perfectly Sir.*

'Just remember you are an officer with naval counter intelligence,' he warned me darkly. 'There are some people who would sell us out, and not just to the Germans.'

We both knew the circles I would be operating in were political, and the individuals I'd be dealing with would each have their own agendas, assessments, plans and projects and most of all contacts; contacts with foreign powers, friendly and unfriendly.

I wasn't naïve, and obviously given his position, neither was my commanding officer. We both knew that HMG would continue to talk to the enemy throughout the war, it was simply the nature of diplomacy. In any conflict channels were always kept open in some way, informally and formally, messages and material passed back and forth.

Whilst at the same time, there would be things we wouldn't talk about to powers who were neutral, friendly, or even allied.

But if HMG was going to be talking to the enemy, then somebody was going to have to do it, and it went without saying that any such contacts would be the subject of the highest levels of concealment.

There's a fine line between diplomacy, high-level contacts, and outright treason, and in wartime that line is drawn under the cover of secrecy. What was being done legitimately, and what was simply people seeking to further their own agendas.

And as far as my old CO was concerned, whatever my official job, part of my ongoing duty as a young naval intelligence lieutenant was to see which side of that line anyone I met was walking. However big a beast they were in the jungle.

*

The more I thought about it back in the office that afternoon, the more sorry I was about having made the stupid 'dodgy dossiers' crack.

Of course, professionally I didn't want to queer my pitch with an important source. But it was more than that.

It was more on the human level. Sir Tom was the sort of 'officer class' Englishman that naturally tended to get my back up. Public school, Oxbridge or Services, with a natural confidence and self-assurance that normally wound me up at the slightest provocation. But he had been kind and given me his time, been charm itself. I had enjoyed speaking to him and it had been a churlish thing to have done to upset him with a cheap shot like that.

I was going to need to ring him again at some point. To apologise

*

I had sat next to R H Bruce Lockhart, a man legendary in intelligence circles from his work in revolutionary Russia. He and the so-called Ace of Spies, Sidney Reilly, had ended up imprisoned in the Kremlin accused of attempting to assassinate Lenin and overthrow the Bolshevik government, only being saved from execution through an exchange of spies. As people settled in along the table awaiting Winston's arrival he had shaken my hand and given me a brief welcome.

'Feel free to ride my coattails for the next couple of days, that way I'll take you round, introduce you to who's who, help you find your feet and so on, then after that you're on your own. How does that sound, alright by you?'

'Thank you, Sir, that's very kind,' I had told him. There hadn't been any need for him to offer to act as a guide if he hadn't wanted to, but there was no denying that a helping hand to find my way around and get up to speed was going to be invaluable.

'That's alright, think nothing of it, we need to get you up and running as quickly as possible, don't we?' he'd replied, before all other conversation had been cut short as we stood up at the Prime Minister entering the room with Eden at his side.

To all intents and purposes it was a meeting of the Joint Intelligence Committee, universally known throughout government by its initials as the JIC. Its membership then as now were the senior officials in the main offices of state, from the Foreign Office, Treasury, Home Office, Ministry of Defence, Ministry of Information and so on, the military chiefs of staff, and the heads of the three Intelligence Services, MI5, MI6 and in those days GC&CS.

As now, the essential role of the JIC was twofold, both to enable the Services to provide their masters and customers with their current intelligence assessments, and for decisions to be made on the priorities and focus of the intelligence agencies work.

And in the case of this particular meeting, the usual attendees were also supplemented with advisors and representatives or specialists from a number of other departments, the two men I'd overheard falling squarely into this capacity.

Once Winston had left, Eden called the meeting to order and announced his agenda.

His intention, he informed us, was the creation of a new coordinating body, the Political Warfare Executive, and he was appointing R H Bruce Lockhart as its Director General.

As cover, the purpose of this group would ostensibly be the

creation and dissemination of propaganda to both support resistance in occupied territory, and to damage enemy morale.

To this end it went on to operate a range of highly effective clandestine radio stations throughout the war which broadcasted reliable but subversive and demoralising information, such as lists of streets and buildings which had been damaged by allied bombing. So successful was this work that after D-Day most of the organisation's staff would be taken over by the Psychological Warfare Division of SHAEF, Supreme Headquarters Allied Expeditionary Force under General Eisenhower.

That was the PWE's overt mission.

Its covert mission, Eden informed us, was to press home the war effort at political and strategic level, and the coordination of all Services, in any way necessary to achieve the desired end.

So to start with, Eden proposed we conduct a quick tour of the horizon. He wanted us to sum up the present position and the key threats we faced, which working outwards he outlined as Sealion, convoys, and the Atlantic, the Mediterranean, and the Far East.

'After which, as we all know,' he told us, 'Winston has given SOE the mission to set Europe ablaze. In line with that our job is as he has just told us, to think the unthinkable, to explore all the options open to us. So, I will be selecting members to form a smaller sub group to take these actions forward.'

And given its purpose, the codename I have selected for this group will be the Press Council.'

*

'And was he helpful?' Dad asked the next day, as I sat at the breakfast table, I wasn't the only one he was feeding. Outside on the window ledge one of the squirrels from the garden was tucking messily into a small pot of muesli Dad had put out. They were tame enough to take it from his hand and I swear some of them came and knocked on the window if there wasn't anything there for them in the morning.

'Oh yes. Everything he told me seems to check out with the other stuff I've seen, both in the files and in what's already been released. Double Cross, Enigma, all that sort of thing.'

'Good. But I of course we'll never really know everything that went on, will we?'

I don't know about how anybody else's family works, but in ours this was one of those ongoing, good natured never-ending debates cum mutual wind ups that Father always returned to.

'More conspiracy theories?' I asked. 'The world doesn't work like that. You can't keep anything that's really big a secret forever, too many people have to know about whatever it is, someone's always bound to talk.'

'Oh, I wouldn't be too sure of that. Look at Enigma,' he said, sliding a plate of croissants onto the table in front of me. 'Jam?'

I nodded, glancing at the papers' headlines. Dad got up early. He'd been up the street to buy the papers and there was already *The Guardian* waiting for me by the coffee. It was all the usual stuff. Another roadside bomb in Iraq. More trouble in Basra.

'There were thousands of people working at Bletchley Park all the way through the war, reading everything the Germans sent, and not a word of it leaked out until when was it, the eighties?'

'Seventies,' I corrected him, 'and yes, but then it did leak, that's my point. Mind you if you did have conspirators they'd have to come up with some better codenames than we used to.'

'Why?'

'Well, I hadn't thought about it much until I was talking to Sir Tom yesterday, but things like Ultra Just make me laugh. Look at the Double Cross system, where they used captured German spies to feedback disinformation to the Nazis. So, what clever codename did they give to the top-secret group that ran it?

'I don't know,' he said, 'What?'

'Only the *Twenty Committee*, after two crosses or XX. Because it means twenty in Latin.'

He laughed, 'Ah, the benefits of a classical education alive and well I see.'

'Incredible isn't it?' I continued, as I spread raspberry jam across a ripped-up croissant, 'the two biggest secrets of the intelligence war for our side were that we could read the German codes and that we had turned all their agents in Britain; and what did we use as code words for them? Ultra and a public schoolboy joke.'

'Who said they were the two biggest secrets?'

'Well they're the biggest that we know about.'

'Precisely. My point exactly.'

I laughed in exasperation, 'And these are the people you think have still got conspiracies concealed?'

That was the thing about conspiracy theories. They made for very good Occam's razors. The simplest explanation of how something had happened was that it was in someone's interest that it had done so. It had a beguiling feel to it, I could understand that.

And let's face it, *cui bono*, who benefits, has always been a good test to apply. If you looked at any event in history and put aside all the cant and rationalisations and stories participants told afterwards to explain it away, you could always just ask yourself who benefited. And if you did that, you sometimes got some very interesting answers.

But in the real world, just because someone benefited, did that mean they had made it happen? That they could ever have even tried to make it happen?

That they could have thought they would be able to control the outcome?

Because only if you thought you could, only if you thought you would actually be sure of benefiting, could you possibly conspire to do anything.

In my view it was just that in the real world, with all its complexity, its competing interests and multifaceted forces, simply trying to trace a clear path of causality, from A to B and through on to C was always fraught with danger and simplifications itself. Without then trying to pin the blame on the machinations of some Mr X behind it all, or some assumption about the power of some small group to ruthlessly manipulate the rest of the world whist remaining hidden in the background. Hidden that is of course except for the traces and tell-tale evidence that those who knew where to look, knew how to join the dots and knew how to fit the pattern together, alone could see.

But then anything that happened was always going to be in someone's interests wasn't it, if you looked hard enough? In any situation someone is always going to benefit somehow. Isn't that what the, *It's an ill wind that blows no one any good* proverb meant?

But just because some outcome had proved to eventually be in someone's interests didn't automatically mean that they had desired it, planned it or even attempted to achieve it. Sometimes the world just works out that way. The world is just too complicated a place to hope to control like that.

Besides which, you could never keep a secret for ever. Even Bletchley Park, Ultra, our ability to read the German Enigma codes, our most closely guarded secret from the end of the war, eventually leaked.

So, three Cs: Complexity, Cock up and Chat. Those were my answers to Dad on conspiracies. You couldn't do it if you wanted to because it was simply too difficult in principle and practise, and even if you did, it would never stay secret for long.

'Are you still looking at Eden?' he asked.

'Yes. It's the right place to start. If we want to write about the interplay between diplomacy and intelligence during the war and afterwards, Eden embodies it. Churchill asked him to take ministerial responsibility for MI5 from 1943 in his personal capacity, while still being Foreign Secretary.'

'And your Sir Tom?'

'I'm not sure he'd like that, but yes I think he's going to be a very useful contact. He seems to have served Eden through much of the war. His name crops up regularly on little committees and stuff in the files.'

'So are you going to try seeing him again?'

'Well, I'm going to do a bit more digging first so I'm better prepared and then I'll try. If he'll see me.'

Which seemed a big if at the time.

'Well, why wouldn't he see you?' Dad asked.

'I made a bloody stupid joke about dodgy dossiers just as I was leaving. I don't think he was amused,' I confessed.

'Well that wasn't very bright now was it, son?'

'No. No it wasn't,' I admitted resignedly.

*

As a representative of Naval Intelligence, it was my responsibility to detail the Service's assessment of Sealion and the fleet's ability to deal with it and so I presented my briefing.

'The Germans have installed coastal batteries with 11-inch, 12-inch and 15-inch guns with an effective range of some fifteen miles, in batteries of four, centred around Griz Nez, and they are working on larger guns that will be capable of hitting Dover.

'We also know from our Ultra intercepts that the German navy will be given a period of ten days before D-Day to lay four minefields, codenames Anton, Bruno, Caesar and Dora to protect the flanks of their invasion fleet.

'And if our ships did get through those, they'll be sitting ducks for the dive bombers. The fleet would be in narrow waters with little room to manoeuvre and Göring's Stuka boys are good and will have overwhelming numbers. It won't matter how many we manage to shoot down, there will still be many more than enough left for the Germans to do the job.'

I looked up as a voice broke the brief silence of my conclusions. It was the man in civvies sounding as ex-Services as he had done earlier.

'So, Winston's right?' he asked bluntly, 'It would be a massacre?'

The resultant arguments took up most of the first hour. A stenographer sat in the corner of the room tapping away at a record of the discussion.

A chap called Maclean, the Foreign Office's expert on economic warfare resources chimed in with his take on the position. 'It takes the Navy three years or more to build a new warship, and that's in peacetime when we have supplies and no one's bombing the hell out of our dockyards. How long is it going to take the Germans to build more Stukas or barges?'

And the arguments ranged from this, the practical, through to the policy level.

'No Gentlemen, it's time to face facts. The Germans want an empire, my question is, so what? We've got one. Why shouldn't they?'

'I'm sorry but you're ignoring years, centuries even, of basic

British foreign policy.'

'Maintenance of the balance of power?'

'Precisely. Never to let a single European power grow that can dominate the continent has been a fundamental plank of British policy ever since the year dot. Britain has always tried to stay out of the fray on the continent. We have kept clear of binding alliances, and have only ever become involved where necessary to help prevent the aggrandisement of a single power on the continent. First it was the Spanish, then it was the French and this century it's the Germans.'

'Now that's all very well in theory, but I'm afraid it seems to me that it's too late. There is a single dominant European power on the continent now, and they're called the Germans. Now it's our duty to deal with the reality of our situation in the country's and the empire's best interests. Choosing to fight a war we cannot possibly win which leads to the loss of our country and empire is frankly recklessness bordering on treasonable dereliction of the government's duties.'

'Survival without honour?'

'Is survival. What use is honour if we have lost the country?'

'So, what do the Germans want?'

'Essentially, what they have already offered us through back channels. Acceptance of their supremacy in continental Europe in return for their acceptance of the British Empire elsewhere round the world, return of the overseas colonies and possessions that they lost in 1919, and our cooperation and assistance in the expulsion of all Jews from their zone of control in Europe.'

'Cooperation and assistance? What do they mean by that?'

Now it was the turn of the Fleet Air Arm officer to speak up.

'Essentially they want to expel all Jews from Western Europe. French Jews would be sent to Madagascar while they would expect us to help in transporting and housing those from Germany, the Netherlands and the Nordic countries, as well all British Jews, who are all to be resettled in Palestine.'

But he didn't find a sympathetic audience, objections coming from right around the table.

'In Palestine? Absolutely impossible!'

'Why?'

'For security of course! For God's sake man. You know we couldn't allow thousands of foreigners into Palestine. Think how close it is to the Suez Canal. No, we simply couldn't take the risk of having such a potential threat to the canal. It's the empire's lifeline man. No, it's simply too much of a risk. We simply couldn't allow it.

'No, the Germans will just have to think of another solution to their Jewish problem.'

And with that Eden announced that we seemed to have covered the ground he wanted us to and it was time to move on to the next subject of convoys and what needed to be done.

By 10:30 we had reached the Mediterranean and the key threat of the Italian fleet in being, currently resting at anchor in Taranto harbour. To which the answer from the First Sea Lord was, 'A solution is in hand. With respect Foreign Secretary but as an operational matter I do not believe it is something for this table, but we've been planning for this eventuality since 1935.'

Eden nodded to signal his agreement. He was, it seemed, keen to make progress, 'Passing on then, finally we come to the Far East…'

*

'So how's it going with your new friends the spooks? Letting you trawl the files, are they?' Dad called from the kitchen where he had put the kettle on as he always did as soon as I, or anyone else for that matter, walked in the door. Nothing had ever been done without a cup of tea being brewed in our house as far as I could recall.

'Great,' I yelled back, as I hung up my coat and headed on through to the back of the house, 'They're being really helpful. Where's Mum?'

I knew she'd want to know about everything I'd been up to. She had taught English in her time and had always wanted to be a writer herself, so when I'd made my decision I'd always known I would have her support and encouragement. Besides which, being a writer is a special thing in an Irish household where words mean so much. Well if you're from that sort of family yourself you won't need me explain it to you.

And if you aren't, I'm not sure I can, which I suppose doesn't say too much about me and my skills in my chosen profession.

'Out gallivanting,' he said, which usually just meant she was up the street shopping, 'With what you see.'

'Yes,' I acknowledged, 'With what they let me see. But they seem to be relatively relaxed about that. If there's something I want to see that I can't then I don't get to see it. It's as simple as that.'

An ex had nicknamed it *the interrogation*, but it just felt a natural part of family life to me, the way my parents always wanted to ask how I was getting on, to understand what I was doing and why. Mind you there was something in her complaints that they each asked the same questions separately although I think her assertion that they only did it so as to be able to compare answers afterwards and check for inconsistencies was going a bit far.

'Really?' Dad sounded a bit sceptical. If I continued to be surprised by what I was being allowed to see and how cooperative the Service had turned out to be about my researches, Dad as an ex civil servant himself was astonished.

I don't think he had yet really got over the idea that the Services would let me through the doors to look at their files at all. He'd taken medical retirement from the Customs thirty years or so ago at a time when I suppose there was quite a different culture in the Civil Service from the one I was now experiencing.

'So it's going well?' he asked, reaching for the teabags as the kettle clicked off.

'Yeah, great thanks. It's early days of course,' I said, as I dumped my bag on the table and pulled out a chair, 'I'm just feeling my way in, worming my way into the files if you like, but I've got some interesting themes starting to emerge already.'

To be honest, I had never thought getting access to their secret files would actually have been so straightforward but then I guessed that they were keen for good PR at the moment to improve their reputations. Stupid crack to make or not, there was no doubt that the dodgy dossier had hurt the Service's reputation.

'And Libby's great.'

'Libby?'

'Short for Elizabeth she tells me.'

I had been introduced to her on my first day at Curzon Street, a slim dark-haired girl in her early twenties, smartly dressed. *Libby here will be looking after you*, I had been told as we shook hands. *She'll be your liaison point for requesting files and information.* Anything I wanted to know, I was to just ask Libby. Although I really didn't think she would tell me anything I wanted to know.

'She's the archivist that I liaise with whenever I want a file from the Registry.'

'Libby the librarian eh?'

*

Sitting to the side of Bruce Lockhart, I heard him confer quietly with Eden, asking, 'Should we reference the Brooke-Popham memo at this point?'

Eden shook his head discretely. 'No, that's not for this meeting.'

Instead the basis of conversation was what is now known as the McCollum memorandum, or the Eight Point Plan. And as Naval Intelligence, it was my job to brief the committee on this as well.

*

Arthur H McCollum had been born in Nagasaki to Baptist Missionary parents. Having graduated from the US Naval Academy in 1923 he had been posted to Japan for three years study, going on to become a key figure in American intelligence in the Pacific and serve as fleet intelligence officer on the staff of Commander in Chief US Fleet during the late 1930s.

Through our sources in Washington, we had somehow been provided with a copy of a memorandum he had written on the 7th October. Entitled *Estimate of the Situation in the Pacific and Recommendations for Action by the United States* it was his assessment of German and Japanese threats to the Unites States.

And it was without doubt, political dynamite.

The two men to whom the memo had been sent gave us some idea of its significance. The first recipient was Captain Dudley

Knox, a man whose somewhat nebulous position as Deputy Director of Naval History belied his levels of personal connections to President Roosevelt dating back to FDR's time as Assistant Secretary of the Navy in the early 1920s, Fleet Admiral Ernest J King, and others at the highest levels of the Navy Department in Washington which made him a highly influential figure behind the scenes. The actual addressee was Walter Stratton Anderson, Director of the Office of Naval Intelligence, a man who reported personally and daily to President Franklin D Roosevelt.

I had arranged for copies of the memo to be included in the folder of papers before each attendee's place setting, every copy numbered for me to checked off as returned against the issue log after the meeting. Given the sensitivity of the memo's contents, as well as our possession of such classified US material only two weeks after it had been penned, at the time it was vital to maintain the security of this information.

Of course, now, having been declassified by the US in 1994, the full text is available for all to see on the internet.

As around the table people began to leaf through the five pages of type, I took them through the key points, while they could gather the detail themselves from the text in their hands.

'As you'll see Gentlemen, McCollum begins by summarising the global position the US finds itself in, …*confronted by a hostile Germany and Italy in Europe and by an equally hostile Japan in the Orient…*' And to him it was looking an increasingly lonely and hostile world.

Russia, the great land link between these two groups of hostile powers, is at present neutral, but in all probability favorably inclined towards the Axis powers, and her favorable attitude towards these powers may be expected to increase in direct proportion to increasing success in their prosecution of the war in Europe.

Germany and Italy have been successful in war on the continent of Europe and all of Europe is either under their military control or has been forced into subservience. Only the British Empire is actively opposing by war the growing world dominance of Germany and Italy and their satellites.

'He considers the USA's attitude towards the war, as well as the attitude of the Axis powers towards America, and the implicit threat he sees this as implying…'

The United States at first remained coolly aloof from the conflict in Europe and there is considerable evidence to support the view that Germany and Italy attempted by every method within their power to foster a continuation of American indifference to the outcome of the struggle in Europe.

Paradoxically, every success of German and Italian arms has led to further increases in United States sympathy for and material support of the British Empire, until at the present time the United States government stands committed to a policy of rendering every support short of war, the changes rapidly increasing that the United States will become a full-fledged ally of the British Empire in the very near future.

The final failure of German and Italian diplomacy to keep the United States in the role of a disinterested spectator has forced them to adopt the policy of developing threats to US security in other spheres of the world, notably by the threat of revolutions in South and Central America by Axis-dominated groups and by the stimulation of Japan to further aggressions and threats in the Far East in the hope that by these means the United States would become so confused in thought and fearful of her own immediate security as to cause her to become so preoccupied in purely defensive preparations as to virtually preclude US aid to Great Britain in any form.

As a result of this policy, Germany and Italy have lately concluded a military alliance with Japan directed against the United States. If the published terms of this treaty and the pointed utterances of German, Italian and Japanese leaders can be believed, and there seems no grounds on which to doubt either, the three totalitarian powers agree to make war on the United States, should she come to the assistance of England, or should she attempt to forcibly interfere with Japan's aims in the Orient and, furthermore, Germany and Italy expressly reserve the right to determine whether American aid to Britain, short of war, is a cause for war or not after they have succeeded in defeating England.

In other words, after England has been disposed of, her enemies will decide whether or not to immediately proceed with an attack on the United States.

Due to geographic conditions, neither Germany nor Italy are in a position to offer any material aid to Japan. Japan, on the contrary, can be of much help to both Germany and Italy by threatening and possibly even attacking British dominions and supply routes from Australia, India and the Dutch East Indies, thus materially weakening Britain's position in opposition to the Axis powers in Europe.

In exchange for this service, Japan receives a free hand to seize all of Asia that she can find it possible to grab, with the added promise that Germany and Italy will do all in their power to keep US attention so distracted as to prevent the United States from taking positive aggressive action against Japan. Here again we have another example of the Axis-Japanese diplomacy which is aimed at keeping American power immobilized, and by threats and alarms to so confuse American thought as to preclude prompt decisive action by the United States in either sphere of action.

It cannot be emphasized too strongly that the last thing desired by either the Axis powers in Europe or by Japan in the Far East is prompt, warlike action by the United States in either theater of operations.

'Next, he reviews what he sees as the USA's options when it comes to its ability to support Britain, as well as and why he believes it is in the fundamental security interests of the USA to support Britain in its struggle in Europe…'

An examination of the situation in Europe leads to the conclusion that there is little that we can do now, immediately, to help Britain that is not already being done.

We have no trained army to send to the assistance of England, nor will we have for at least a year.

We are now trying to increase the flow of materials to England and to bolster the defence of England in every practicable way and this aid will undoubtedly be increased.

On the other hand, there is little that Germany or Italy can do against us as long as England continues in the war and her navy maintains control of the Atlantic.

The one danger to our position lies in the possible early defeat of the British Empire with the British fleet falling intact into the hands of the Axis powers. The possibility of such an event occurring would be materially lessened were we actually allied in war with the British or at the very least were taking active measures to relieve the pressure on Britain in other spheres of action.

To sum up: the threat to our security in the Atlantic remains small so long as the British fleet remains dominant in that ocean and friendly to the United States.

'Given his position in the US intelligence community, unsurprisingly he turns to the Pacific. As you will see gentlemen, he discusses how the threat of Japanese aggression could affect the war in Europe. His interest here is clearly around the ability of the British Empire to survive and continue to act as a bulwark for the US in the Atlantic, as well as by implication the ability of the US to maintain pressure on Japan to control any threat to the Americans in the region...'

In the Pacific, Japan by virtue of her alliance with Germany and Italy is a definite threat to the security of the British Empire and once the British Empire is gone, the power of Japan-Germany and Italy is to be directed against the United States.

A powerful land attack by Germany and Italy through the Balkans and North Africa against the Suez Canal with a Japanese threat or attack on Singapore would have very serious results for the British Empire.

Could Japan be diverted or neutralized, the fruits of a successful attack on the Suez Canal would not be as far reaching and beneficial to the Axis powers as if such a success was also accompanied by the virtual elimination of British sea power from the Indian Ocean, thus opening up a European supply route for Japan and a sea route for Eastern raw materials to reach Germany and Italy. Japan must be diverted if the British and American blockade of Europe and possibly Japan is to remain even partially in effect.

The initial conclusion of his analysis was that *while there is little that the United States can do to immediately retrieve the situation in Europe, the United States is able to effectively nullify Japanese aggressive action, and do it without lessening US material assistance to Great Britain.*

'He sets out in point form a high-level assessment of the strengths and weakness of Japan's strategic position, and then that of the US, noting that, *In the Pacific the United States possesses a very strong defensive position and a navy and naval air force at present in that ocean capable of long distance offensive operation,* as well as listing... *other factors which at the present time are strongly in our favor...,* such as potentially friendly Dutch, British and Chinese forces and territories.

'His military conclusions from this are stark...'

A consideration of the foregoing leads to the conclusion that prompt aggressive naval action against Japan by the United States would render Japan incapable of affording any help to Germany and Italy in their attack on England and that Japan itself would be faced with a situation in which her navy could be forced to fight on most unfavourable terms or accept fairly early collapse of the country through the force of blockade.

A prompt and early declaration of war after entering into suitable arrangements with England and Holland would be most effective in bringing about the early collapse of Japan, and thus eliminating our enemy in the pacific before Germany and Italy could strike at us effectively.

Furthermore, elimination of Japan must surely strengthen Britain's position against Germany and Italy and, in addition, such action would increase the confidence and support of all nations who tend to be friendly towards us.

'However, his political conclusions are equally succinct, if substantially less favourable to us...'

It is not believed that in the present state of political opinion the United States government is capable of declaring war against Japan without more ado; and it is barely possible that vigorous action on our part might lead the Japanese to modify their attitude.

'As a result, he goes on to propose an eight-point plan in respect of actions the United States should take to deal with the Japanese threat...'

Therefore, the following course of action is suggested:

A. Make an arrangement with Britain for the use of British bases in the Pacific, particularly Singapore.

B. Make an arrangement with Holland for the use of base facilities and acquisition of supplies in the Dutch East Indies.

C. Give all possible aid to the Chinese government of Chiang-Kai-Shek.

D. Send a division of long range heavy cruisers to the Orient, Philippines, or Singapore.

E. Send two divisions of submarines to the Orient.

F. Keep the main strength of the US fleet now in the Pacific in the vicinity of the Hawaiian Islands.

G. Insist that the Dutch refuse to grant Japanese demands for undue economic concessions, particularly oil.

H. Completely embargo all US trade with Japan, in collaboration with a similar embargo imposed by the British Empire.

'But I'd suggest it's his final paragraph which makes the most interesting reading gentlemen as I feel it leaves us, and his readers in Washington, in no doubt about where he believes the situation in the Pacific is inevitably leading...'

If by these means Japan could be led to commit an overt act of war, so much the better. At all events we must be fully prepared to accept the threat of war.

Chapter 4

The general opinion here, that an invasion will be attempted in the near future, has grown ground.

Reuters New Agency, London, 14 September 1940

'So gentlemen,' I concluded, once everyone had caught their breath, 'McCollum's summary reads:

1. The United States is faced by a hostile combination of powers in both the Atlantic and Pacific.

2. British naval control of the Atlantic prevents hostile action against the United States in this area.

3. Japan's growing hostility presages an attempt to open sea communications between Japan and the Mediterranean by an attack on the British lines of communication in the Indian Ocean.

4. Japan must be diverted if British opposition in Europe is to remain effective.

5. The United States naval forces now in the Pacific are capable of so containing and harassing Japan as to nullify her assistance to Germany and Italy.

6. It is to the interest of the United States to eliminate Japan's threat in the Pacific at the earliest opportunity by taking prompt and aggressive action against Japan.

7. In the absence of United States ability to take the political offensive, additional naval force should be sent to the Orient and agreements entered into with Holland and England that would serve as an effective check against Japanese encroachments in South-Eastern Asia.

I put down my papers and resuming my seat, waited for questions.

'Do we know anything about how the Americans are taking this?' Hugh asked from down the table.

'All we have is a note appended to it by Captain Knox,' I told him. 'He doesn't seem to disagree with the analysis as such, but he does appear to be a bit cautious on following through on the proposed actions.'

> *It is unquestionably to our general interest that Britain be not licked – just now she has a stalemate and probably can't do better. We ought to make it certain that she at least gets a stalemate. For this she will probably need from us substantial further destroyers and air reinforcements to England. We should not precipitate anything in the Orient that should hamper our ability to do this – so long as probability continues.*

> *If England remains stable, Japan will be cautious in the Orient. Hence our assistance to England in the Atlantic is also protection to her and us in the Orient.*

> *However, I concur in your courses of action, we must be ready on both sides and probably strong enough to care for both.*

'So, the yanks want to give us just enough to keep going, is that it?' was Hugh's bitter sounding question.

'Well at least they want to do that…' someone started, before Hugh cut them off angrily.

'But it's not just enough is it?' he said, 'It never is, is it?'

*

August 2007

It was coming up to lunchtime on Wednesday as I left their discreet offices on Curzon Street. It was one of the anonymous old buildings that they didn't use any more operationally ever since they had moved out of their old headquarters at Century House on Westminster Bridge Road and consolidated all their London operations into Legoland at Vauxhall Cross, so they had set it up for use as the reading room.

Really, it was a bit early to knock off, but I'd gone through the files I'd had out today, and I had filled out the dockets with my requests for the next ones I wanted to see, so there wasn't much more I could do. Assuming my requests were approved, the papers wouldn't be delivered from the Registry archive until tomorrow morning. I had thought about popping across to the British Library and the reading room there but decided it could wait until next Monday when I would be coming back down and arriving at Euston mid-morning anyway. It wasted some time getting into town that late I knew, but I could work on the way and tickets were slightly less extortionate for trains into

London after rush hour.

So I followed my usual routine. A quick cut through the back streets to grab a sandwich from Shepherd's Market and then up Piccadilly to hop on the tube at Green Park; a few stops on the Jubilee line to Waterloo and half an hour or so on the Woking train down to Weybridge. It was a nice day so I'd probably stretch my legs and walk down the hill and through town to Mum and Dad's where later I would have a session up in the converted attic room writing up my notes.

There was plenty of room. My brothers and I had grown up here, but now as one was in the USA and the other was up North, there was just Mum and Dad, other than when the families descended during the school holidays with my nephews and nieces.

I was feeling good after two weeks or so divided between here, the National Archives at Kew where the Service deposited files twice a year, the Foreign Office, and the British Library. A fortnight of wading through files and reading papers, scanning books and scribbling notes to be puzzled over later and I felt I was at last starting to see the wood for the trees. A main theme was emerging, starting to solidify in my mind as the central spine running through what I was seeing. It was a thread that brought many of the different aspects together, but one robust enough for me to hang our first episode around, as well as being the lead into the accompanying book I already had my mind on.

I picked up my phone and laptop from the cloakroom at reception. I was allowed to take a pad of paper into the reading room and to make notes to bring out again, but not to bring anything electronic in. They were very clear about the rules. My clearance to see files for research did not necessarily extend to any of the documents being cleared to be released more generally. So, if I wanted a copy of something I'd read, I could ask and they would then consider whether it could be allowed and if so, they would prepare one for me. In fact so far, there hadn't been a problem with anything that I'd wanted to copy. But then again, at this early stage of my research there hadn't been many documents I felt I actually needed to keep. I was reading my way in I suppose, trying to get an overview, the big picture, and as I say, just starting to see what was emerging from the detail.

I slipped the laptop into my rucksack along with my notes and as I hitched it over my shoulder and pushed my way out through the front door into the bright London sunlight I switched my phone on. There were no messages, no calls waiting which was fine, if a little odd. I would give Dad a quick bell to let him know I was on my way.

As I walked off down the street I still couldn't quite believe it. That I was actually after all these years on the verge of making a huge success of doing what I had, ever since I could remember, always wanted to do.

This series was going to be big. I just knew it in my bones.

*

'Nevertheless,' someone argued, 'at least it shows at a senior level they realise the stakes and where their interests lie.'

Hugh nodded in seemingly reluctant agreement. 'Well we could pick up on some of his suggestions, I suppose. Why not look at sending some of our capital ships on a tour? Fly the flag, show of force? We could visit the Americans. Seeing the assets we have in place like the *Prince of Wales* or the *Repulse* could give them a bit of encouragement?'

There was a murmur of agreement around the table which Eden approved. 'It's an interesting idea certainly,' before turning to me to make a note. 'Let's explore the practicalities, shall we?'

'We'll need to ensure the security of all the ports we might want them to visit,' observed Hugh. 'Can we get something on that?'

Again Eden nodded his agreement and passed the task across to me with an instruction to supply Hugh with the details. And having in effect formed a small sub group of Hugh and myself to coordinate this project Eden announced that having covered off this initial review of the four key theatres, perhaps it was time to take a short break for tea and could we resume in say twenty minutes.

*

As some took the opportunity to stretch their legs and others visited the head, others gathered in clusters to sip their tea and continue the discussions. Deliberately I joined the knot of half a dozen or so at the far end of the room which included Bruce Lockhart and Hugh.

'Right, that's agreed then. Now, what's next on the agenda?'

one of them speculated.

'A two-front war?'

'Oh really? Who do you have in mind, us or someone else?'

'What about the Americans coming in on our side?'

'You are joking, aren't you? Hugh barked angrily. You've just heard what McCollum had to say haven't you? And he's right. There was a poll back in May. Only seven percent of Americans were in favour of entering the war on the side of us and France. Now France has fallen, do you really think they're going to be any keener? Particularly with that shit Kennedy here as ambassador.'

'I know, him running around telling FDR that he only gives us a few weeks doesn't help.'

The truth was, leaving Joe Kennedy aside, everyone in the room knew how strong a force American isolationism was.

Earlier that summer life sized effigies of senators thought to be in favour of intervention had been strung up from oak trees across the way from Capitol Hill, before being dragged through the streets behind cars. An enraged mothers' movement lynch-mob prowled Washington DC dressed in mourning black, protesting at calls for compulsory military training and accusing congress of plotting to kill their sons. Senator Robert Taft declared FDR's big government policies were a good deal more dangerous than Nazism, congressmen called each other traitor and war profiteers as fist fights broke out in the House of Representatives, while across the country the world-famous aviator Charles Lindbergh toured the country promoting the America First Committee's campaign against the supply of aid to Britain.

'No. There is no way that America is going to drop its isolationist stance.' I had to admit I thought Hugh was right on that.

'Winston puts a lot of faith in FDR,' someone objected.

But Hugh was having none of it. 'FDR's a politician. He's up to his eyes in an election and facing strong isolationist and strong pro German lobbies. Besides which, why join a side that you think is going to lose?'

'Well....'

'Not to mention the fact that FDR is actively hostile to the whole idea of the British Empire. No, the United States is not going to war to save, or be seen to be saving, our Empire.'

Somebody raised the Tizard mission which had finally taken place the previous month. Following a soul-searching decision by Churchill, Tizard and his team had packed a trunk with the details of all our latest technology, from the cavity magnetron for radar and the design of a new type of engine by Frank Whittle, through to the Frisch-Peieris memorandum on the feasibility of an atomic weapon, and right down to specification of plastic explosives, superchargers and self-sealing fuel tanks, stuck it on a train to Liverpool docks and sailed to the US. Partly it was an attempt to win them over, partly it was an acknowledgement that whilst we needed much of this equipment, we simply didn't have the resources to manufacture it for ourselves, and so passing the designs and information across to the Americans if they would make it, was the only option we had left.

Not needless to say, that Hugh saw it that way.

'We're trying to bribe them in, and it just won't work...'

'Oh come on...' someone started to protest.

'Well what else do you call it?' Hugh snapped. 'Even when we do give them all the goodies in the shop, what do we get back for it? Fifty clapped out destroyers, that's what,' he fumed. 'We're giving them everything we have and they're selling us the minimum.'

'So what's your solution?' somebody challenged him.

'Mine? You know what mine is, same as the Soviet Union, we have to force them in.'

'And how on earth would we do that?'

'He's not going to tell you that, now is he?' said Bruce Lockhart, smiling as he sipped his tea.

'Not even here?'

'No,' Bruce Lockhart replied, as Hugh kept his silence and a look passed between them, 'Hugh here, doesn't trust anyone, do you Hugh?'

'This is a group of Cabinet Office advisors for God's sake,' came an affronted voice in a tone of outraged entitlement that I couldn't help but have to stifle a smile at. 'Are you saying he doesn't trust the discretion of the people in this room?

Hugh's eyes were scanning the group, and I noticed his eyes had lit on my uniform and proximity to Bruce Lockhart. It was as though I could feel him assessing my position.

But it was Bruce Lockhart who jokingly let Hugh off the hook. 'Anyway, I for one would rather not know, given the sorts of things that go on in Hugh's head.'

'But our chaps are starting to try to hit back surely? Bombing raids...' someone else said, changing the subject.

'Well of course we know all about that, don't we...' said Hugh jumping in.

But what he said next shocked me. Charlie had never breathed a word about it on any of the times he'd been home on leave. Well I suppose we were a family which could keep secrets after all.

'The problem our boys have is that our equipment is rubbish. They can't hit a barn door at twenty paces with the bombsights we have. The yanks on the other hand have the Norden, they can drop a bomb into a barrel from twenty thousand feet and be back home for pancakes.

'We're giving them our future. Our most precious secrets. Tizard's taken his briefcase chock full of goodies, and what have we had in return? Do they even give us a bombsight? Not a chance, so our chaps just have to carry on risking their lives every time they go up to waste their time with what they have over there.

'It makes me sick!' he announced, discarding his empty cup on the sideboard.

And it made me sick just listening to him. And thinking about Charlie.

The Norden bombsight. It was the first time I'd heard of it, and as I was later to discover through some judicious digging, it was absolutely true what he was saying. At the time it was undoubtedly the best there was in the world, and the Americans wouldn't share it with us. Not then, and not later in the war when we were allies. It remained an American secret right to the end with even FDR unable to deliver it.

The traffic in technology in secrets was a one-way street from us to them.

Still, as I saw it at the time, that was just the price we had to pay. *Bribery* Hugh called it. Buying influence and goodwill at the highest level might be another way of describing it.

*

Back in the office, the producer was fuming.

She'd obviously had some kind of a row with a manager before I'd got in for our progress meeting to brief her on where I'd got to. From the rant I'd heard as I unpacked my gear I gathered it was something about the BBC top brass, and what Auntie might, or might not, want to see put out.

'Licence renewal, it's always sodding licence renewal, or worry about the governors and what the politicians are going to do...' she was moaning. It must have been a full-on *Death on the Rock* conversation.

So while she had her sponsors, that didn't mean the whole of the corporation was automatically behind her project. She was being leant on by someone. It wasn't that unusual a thing to happen, whether about the substance of the concept or by someone looking to advance their own rival pitch. I was just glad it was something which went on way above my pay grade.

'Yes, well you know it's always politics,' I sympathised noncommittally. But however angry she felt, she needed to be careful for all our sakes. With as high profile a project as this I knew it was all our jobs on the block here if it ever became an issue.

One thing you quickly learnt in an organisation like this was, shit also rolls downhill.

*

Our twenty-minute break was nearly up and people were starting to gravitate back towards their places around the table.

'So who was that?' I asked Bruce Lockhart quietly, as we sat down.

'Who? Oh, that's Hugh. Very very senior in the Service. Why?'

'Well I just wanted to check something with you...' I told him.

During the break Hugh's friend, the Fleet Air Arm officer, had taken the opportunity to introduce himself to me as Sempill. Then he'd gone on to ask if I could send him a copy of the briefing I'd been instructed to prepare for Hugh, once it was ready. It seemed an odd request as I couldn't see what it would have to do with the Fleet Air Arm, but he had mumbled something about having had experience in the Pacific, and some suggestion that in casting an eye over whatever I produced, he might be able to help fill in any gaps.

Bruce Lockhart's advice was blunt when I asked him what he thought. 'Don't give it to him, I don't trust him.'

He swiftly checked to see if we could be overheard, before he continued.

'A word to the wise, I'd steer clear of Sempill if I were you,' he told me in that professional Civil Service murmur as he slipped an unrationed lump of sugar into his refill of tea he'd brought back to the table with him.

'Why?' I asked quietly.

'Because he's known for the company he keeps. He's always been an admirer of generalissimos.'

Before the war it seemed Sempill had been well known for his involvement in the Right Club, the Anglo-German Fellowship, and the pro-Nazi Link organisation, whose head Admiral Sir Barry Domvile was currently languishing in well-deserved internment.

Appalled. I wanted to ask, *What the hell was he doing at a meeting like this*? But I hadn't heard the worst of it.

Japan had been on our side in the Great War and we stayed in a formal alliance afterwards. By 1920, the Air Ministry and Foreign Office had seen Japan as a potentially lucrative market for arms deals and after the Japanese had started to buy British flying boats, Sempill as an expert on seaplanes had led a trade delegation of fellow retired naval air officers to advise them on setting up the Imperial Japanese Navy's air service.

The mission was a great success, described as 'almost epoch-making' in a personal thank you letter from Japan's then Prime Minister, Katō Tomosaburo.

All of which discussions about technology and tactics should have come to an abrupt halt with the end of the alliance in 1921. Sempill however evidently had other ideas, and back home in Britain whilst continuing to work on facilitating foreign trade missions to British aircraft factories, he went on to maintain contact through Captain Teijirō Toyoda, Naval attaché at the Japanese embassy in London, and intelligence officer.

Unbeknownst to Sempill however, all his communications with Toyoda had been under surveillance since 1922 and MI5 were tapping his phone. Soon they had evidence that he was passing information on British aircraft development to Toyoda, simply relaying the answers he'd gathered on his factory visits to questions he'd been asked to put, in return for significant sums of money, while his valet was in fact a serving Japanese seaman.

It was only when the Aviation Ministry proposed him for an appointment as Greece's aeronautical adviser in March 1926 that MI5 warned the Foreign Office against this on the basis of Sempill's past activities.

He was called into the Foreign Office for an interview to try to establish where his loyalties lay and how much he had passed across to the Japanese. But without giving the game away about how much they already knew, all they were actually able to challenge him on was the fact he'd been overheard by a civil servant talking on the train about a classified new aircraft and Sempill had to admit he had broken the Official Secrets Act.

'But why the hell wasn't he prosecuted?' I wanted to know.

Bruce Lockhart just shrugged.

'Not in HMG's interests. Far too embarrassing for one thing. His father was George V's aide-de-camp at the time. But the interviewer couldn't go in too far, as it could also have tipped off the Japanese about where we'd got to on their codes.'

As I digested that, I was left to wonder, if all that was true, why had Sempill been appointed to the Department of Air Matériel at the Admiralty? A post that would give him access to almost all aspects of information about our naval aircraft and weapons development.

And why on earth had he been allowed to be privy to what I'd just been briefing on?

'But then Hugh has also asked me to give it to him…' I said.

'Well that settles it,' he observed grimly. 'Under no circumstances.'

'Why?'

'Sempill and Hugh are natural allies. Sempill is pro the Japs,' he told me.

'And Hugh?'

'Well you've just heard why not Hugh. He just hates the yanks.'

I had just been informally warned off Hugh and Sempill as security risks. The two men I'd overheard conferring about the need for terms before the meeting was even underway.

But just then Eden announced 'Gentlemen, please…' and so we resumed our seats.

*

Out of interest, prompted by some of Sir Tom's comments, the next day I had asked Libby for some files on the operations and committees where I thought he would have been involved. As I read through these over the next week or so I found it was all good background stuff of itself, helping me to round out a picture of some of the things he had been involved in during the war, so it wasn't a waste of time. But it also gave me some loose ends that were worth following up. It was an excuse to call him really.

Sitting in a coffee bar on my lunch break early the following week I dialled his number. The phone rang about three times before it connected and his precise voice came on the line.

'Hello, can I help you?'

'Hello Sir Tom,' I said, reintroducing myself. 'We spoke last month.'

He made polite noises. 'Oh yes, of course.'

'Anyway,' I said, plunging on and hoping that the momentum would carry the conversation through, 'I hope you don't mind me ringing again.'

'Well…'

'It's just that I had a few follow-up questions that I wanted to ask you if you had a moment, and…'

'And?'

'And I just wanted to say sorry as well.'

'Sorry? Oh thank...' Sir Tom sounded surprised, but then he checked himself.

'For what?' he asked.

'For the crack about the dodgy dossier. I thought it I had upset you.'

There was a moment's silence from the other end of the line.

'Oh, for that.'

There was a pause. Had I called at a bad time I wondered, he sounded distracted? Should I offer to call back?

'No,' he said at last.

Then he spoke again in a stronger voice. 'No, don't worry about that.'

'Well, thank you. Is it convenient to talk at the moment?' I asked, 'I can call back later if you'd prefer?'

Again, there seemed a hesitation in his voice, but then he said, 'No, it's fine. I've plenty of time. What can I help you with?'

We spoke for about half an hour or so. As before we ranged widely and he was generally and genuinely very helpful.

That was, until I started to touch on some areas relating to his work in 1940 and 1941 with Eden. One of his jobs seemed to have been on something called the Press Commission. I hadn't seen any records of its meetings but it looked as though it had something to do with censorship as it appeared, from what I could work out, to fall under the umbrella of both the D Notice Committee and the PWE.

So I was a bit surprised by how sharply he reacted when I asked him about it in passing.

'Oh really?' he said sharply, 'Well, there shouldn't be much of a mystery about that I wouldn't have thought. The Press Commission came within the remit of the PWE after all. We worked with each of the key newspapers of the day on censorship, about the policies on what could and couldn't be published. The D notices then enforced the detail on a day to day basis.'

'Oh, I see...' I was disappointed somehow that it seemed so obvious as soon as he said it, but there it was, I supposed.

He had evidently decided that this line of questioning had gone far enough.

'I don't think I can help you any more on this I'm afraid. And listen, I don't want to be rude, but I'm afraid I'm going to have to go now.'

'Of course, Sir Tom,' I said, a bit surprised by the sudden turn the conversation had taken, 'Well thank you for your time and I'm sorry to have disturbed you.'

We said our farewells quickly. He obviously wanted me off the line and fast.

I wondered what I had done to upset him this time?

Chapter 5

All warfare is based upon deception.

Sun Tzu, The Art of War

The next day when I arrived at Curzon Street, there was a different atmosphere.

I checked in as normal, showed my pass at the desk and handed over my bag and phone to the commissionaire's office.

But then, rather than the commissionaire calling through for Libby to come and escort me along to the reading room, I was asked to take a seat in the lobby and wait.

I didn't have to sit there long. After no more than a few minutes a rather short, stocky man who looked to be in his forties appeared wearing a dark suit, a fixed smile and a shock of sandy ginger hair, and escorted me into a small anonymous looking interview room behind an equally anonymous looking door just off the hallway.

We sat down across a Civil Service issue Formica table and after a few pleasantries he came swiftly to the point. I was given a gentle but firm warning not to try to pursue any lines of enquiry using the classified files that I was being given access to which went beyond the remit of what had been agreed with the Service that I would be researching.

'It's not a big deal, mate,' he said, leaning back casually in his chair having delivered his piece, 'but we can't have you going on a fishing trip through our files, now can we? You understand that I suppose. And I have just had word come down from the top that there are places that they don't want you going.'

So I wasn't being barred from researching. It wasn't anything as crude or final as that. But it was very clear that I'd just been given a warning short across the bows.

But the problem was however, about what? I was mystified.

I had been cleared to investigate deception, intelligence and diplomacy during the war years. As Sir Tom had said there was a huge amount of material on everything from Ultra to the Double Cross system now in the public domain. So, I was really at a loss to understand why any of my questions yesterday would have caused any concern.

Because one other thing was clear as well. It had to have been Sir Tom. He must have made contact with the Service and told them what I had been asking about.

The thing was though, I couldn't understand why. As far as I could see the stuff that I had been asking him about was all fairly innocuous. To be honest, I couldn't see what all the fuss was about.

And what's more, the officer across the table from me didn't seem to be too sure either.

'So can you tell me what's off limits?' I asked, seeking clarification.

'No, I can't really.'

'Why not?'

'Well, then it's a known unknown isn't it?' he said smiling calmly at me. 'If we tell you what you can't look at, we're telling you something aren't we?'

'But I can still look at cleared papers?'

'Well yes, obviously,' he said expansively.

'So how do I know if I'm treading on ground you don't want me to?'

'Well I guess we'll just have to tell you, won't we?'

'But won't it then become a known unknown?' I asked.

'Not if we can help it,' he smiled again. Now this was someone whose arrogance was getting my goat and I was already tired of his Cheshire Cat impression. The bastard's enjoying this, I thought.

*

A commissionaire escorted me along the corridor and down to the reading room where Libby was waiting for me. She had an armful of buff cardboard files from the last of the day before yesterday's request sheets that she carried over to the desk I used as I plonked my notebook down.

'Have I got you into trouble somehow?' I asked quietly, as I pulled out the chair.

'I don't know,' she said, 'I don't think so. I have been asked what files you've asked to see and which ones I've shown you. I'm not sure what the problem is but I'm in the clear, I've only ever given you files that have been cleared for you.'

'Are there many that aren't?'

'Some.'

'What, from the war?'

'Yes.'

'Many?'

'Oh yes, I would think so.'

I was surprised at that, 'What, still now, all these years later?'

'Yes.'

'But why?'

'Why?' she shrugged, 'I can't tell you that, and even if I could...'

'You wouldn't?'

'That's right. You know the rules. Now if that's all, what can I help you with today?'

Well today, I thought, if the Security Service didn't mind too much, I'd like to have another look at some of the D Notice and Press Commission stuff where I'd seen Sir Tom's name come up. Whatever it was that I'd strayed too close to, something like censorship was surely reasonably safe ground? If I plugged away at that for a while I thought, perhaps the fuss would die down a bit. Anyway, whatever it had been that they had been concerned about, for the life of me I couldn't see what the issue could be. The war had been over for more than sixty years, so what could anyone possibly care about now?

Except Sir Tom cared about something I presumed, as Libby walked away to check the Registry index to see what was available in the files on some of the meetings and records I'd requested. So the question really was, why?

What, I asked myself, did I actually know about Sir Tom, about his later war and peacetime record? He had evidently been a senior spook, but there was something else about him I guessed that I needed to know.

Come to think about it, I didn't know as much about Libby as I wanted to either. So perhaps it was time to try and do something about that too, I decided.

'Fancy a coffee?' I asked as I wandered up to her desk by the door an hour or so later and returned the first files she had given me. 'We can go for plastic in the canteen or proper stuff in the real world outside. It's up to you.'

'Oh, go on then,' she said, 'I could do with a breath of fresh air for a few minutes. I'll just call Janet to take over and I'll be with you.'

*

In the cold sunshine we wandered towards a bench in Green Park, sipping our takeaway lattes.

'Christ it's depressing,' I said, as I pushed aside some fallen leaves and an abandoned *Metro* with its headline about more casualties in Iraq.

'Isn't it just,' she agreed, 'How many is it saying?'

'Another one dead and two seriously wounded,' I read, as I folded it in half and stuck it in a bin beside the bench.

'But you are in the Service?' I asked as we sat down.

'Yes. But I'm not an officer or anything.'

'So you're not a spook?'

'Me?' she laughed at the idea, 'Oh no!'

'So what are you then?'

'Well, I'm a librarian,' she said.

'Really, a librarian?' I smiled, Dad had been right after all, 'You're kidding me?'

'No, I'm not, honestly. I've got a degree in Modern History and then I did a Masters in Librarianship at Cardiff. They needed an archivist to organise stuff for researchers. There's the Registry staff but they are all tied up on operational stuff so they put out an ad for a graduate data officer and well, here I am.'

'Wow! So who would have thought being a librarian could be so exciting?'

She laughed, 'Not me for a start.'

*

Over the next week I tried to stay focused but I couldn't help it. Everywhere I looked, each piece of research material I found, every file I pulled all seemed inexorably to lead back in one direction. Towards what Eden and his intelligence liaison, Lieutenant Tom Belvoir, were doing during the war.

The censorship angle seemed particularly odd, I thought, although for the life of me, I couldn't see where else it might lead.

As I'd already discovered, they had both been on something called the Press Commission from when it had been formed in late 1940. Eden had chaired it which seemed to be a bit of a low-level job for him, given what else he had on in his brief at the time; while Sir Tom, or Lieutenant T Belvoir RN, as he was at the time, had been the Commission's secretary from the outset. From what I could see in the files, it came under the auspices of the PWE which Eden also chaired and seemed to have some overall remit for the Press in connection with the war. But what exactly its role was or why it had been formed was difficult to tell as none of the files were available.

'Not available?' I asked Libby.

'No,' she said briskly.

'Why not? Don't tell me they're still classified,' I joked.

'No. They're just not listed in the index.'

'Which means?'

'I'm not sure to be honest,' she said. 'It could be that they've been lost, we do have some gaps you know, and the minutes of some ad hoc committee on censorship...'

'It was hardly that, with Eden chairing,' I protested.

'...might not have survived,' she continued, 'Either that, or...'

'Or?'

'They are still classified.'

'But you just said they weren't.'

'No, I didn't,' she corrected me, 'I just said they're not on the list of files in the index where I would see them as classified ones. But then the highest graded secret files would not be on the normal classified registry.'

Now this was news, I thought. 'Wouldn't they?'

'No. There's a top-level registry for the most sensitive information.'

It made sense, I supposed. As my friendly interviewer had pointed out, *unknown unknowns* were a lot more secure than *known unknowns*; and so excluding the most sensitive files from the least secure registry was a logical enough way of restricting knowledge about top secret items to the more senior levels who presumably needed to know.

'Do you have access to it?' I teased.

'No, of course I don't,' she said, 'I haven't got that sort of level of clearance. And you know it!'

'Can you ask about it?'

'Yes, I suppose I could, if you wanted me to.'

I thought about that for a moment. I'd just had one brush with the Service for straying off my reservation. And so, asking to go ploughing through the most secret registry index on the trail of Sir Tom didn't seem like a particularly smart move to make just at that point.

'No. No that's OK,' I said reluctantly, as discretion got the better part of valour. 'It would just seem odd you know. That something about censorship could still be that secret even now.'

'That's if it is, of course,' she pointed out caustically, 'As I say it might just be that the files are missing, or there may not have been files at all.'

'But if there were files? Why would they be so secret? And I keep coming back to why would Eden and Sir Tom be involved in something like censorship?' I wondered out loud.

'Well that's not necessarily so strange when you think about it,' she pointed out. 'To ensure that your censorship is working you have to know what needs to be covered or hushed up, don't you? So you need someone in overall charge who has sufficient access and knowledge about what is really going on to be able to make a judgement about what should and shouldn't be released.'

It made sense I supposed, and was also potentially quite a powerful position to have as well, deciding what would and would not be revealed to the people. For some reason the image of Winston Smith at work creating, and then recreating acceptable history in his cubicle at Minitrue came to mind and I started to see why perhaps it needed to be controlled by someone at Eden's sort of level.

'And then of course you had a strong connection with the MI5 Double Cross system,' she continued, 'Where you're carrying out a systematic deception of the enemy you're going to need to control what information and misinformation get fed into the Press for the enemy to pick up.'

And I knew that was true. MI5 and the government had made active use of the Press when necessary as part of their deception operations. With agent Zig Zag they had staged a fake sabotage plot to blow up the power supplies to the De Havilland plant at Hatfield where the Mosquito was built. As part of that operation they had planted a brief report of the explosion in the Press, which was then rapidly suppressed in the way a real incident would have been, to make the whole thing seem real.

*

So if help from the US was out of the question, then this seemed to leave us with only one other option.

As Eden put it to open the discussion, 'Gentlemen, we all know that Germany does not want a war on two fronts. German war planning for the Great War was based on this idea, envisaging a quick knockout blow in the West enabling them to quickly turn to face the threat from the East before Russia could become organised. And in the last twenty years, nothing much about the German central strategic problem has changed.'

'Other than the fact that they have knocked France out with a quick blow and aren't at war with Russia,' came an objection.

'Well yes, but they are still at war with us in the West and pact or no pact, everything the Nazis have ever said about Bolshevism leads you to think that war in the East is going to come sooner or later.'

'Why?'

'*Lebensraum*. It's the key to Hitler's world view. If you read

Mein Kampf he spells it out clearly, Germany needs living room and its destiny is in expansion in the East.'

'So?'

'So what I want to discuss is what our views on this prospect should be.'

'Let the Nazis and the Bolsheviks fight it out I say.'

'And have one emerge stronger than the other? That doesn't sound an attractive prospect.'

'Well there are a number of options aren't there? We could make peace with Germany.'

'Are you mad?'

'Look, I'm not suggesting it, but if we're going to do our job properly we need to have all the options on the table.'

'Well, very well then.'

'The Nazis had always said that they did not want war with us.'

'Not the *Britain is not our natural enemy* thing again?'

'Yes, that again. Hitler has always said how much he admires the British Empire. So, as I say, we could make peace with Germany along the lines that were already offered.'

'We keep the Empire and they have a free hand in Europe?'

'Yes. In that case we, the country and the empire survive. If there's no war between Russia and Germany, well, we are no worse off. However if there is, then we have to realise that a part of our deal with Germany is likely to be that we will need to decide to become involved.'

'Fight on the German side against the Russians?'

'Is the idea really so farfetched? Don't forget that we were intervening in the civil war right up until 1920, with Winston's full support. We've got Operation Pike lined up as a strategic bombing plan focused on destroying their Caucasian oil fields, and only back in February we were planning to send a hundred thousand to support Finland against the Russians. It was just because the Swedes and Norwegians wouldn't cooperate on transit rights that we didn't, otherwise we'd probably be at war right now.'

'But what if the Germans win?'

'Then we run the risk that she will have become even stronger. She will have all of Russia's vast natural resources of food, minerals and oil to exploit.'

'What if we don't make peace?'

'Well if there's no war with Russia, then at least the threat of one keeps troops tied up in Poland and Prussia which can't be used against us. On the other hand, we know that Russia is supplying the German military machine with huge amounts of raw materials so peace in the East is actively working against us.'

'Will the Germans attack Russia anyway?'

'Possibly. We believe there's a school of thought at the top that thinks that the only reason we haven't surrendered is because we are waiting for a Russo/German war to break out and that a quick defeat of Russia would then give us no option but to give in.'

'So they think if they defeat Russia we'll give up, is that it? Because they can then turn all their forces against us?'

'That's the theory.'

'So what is the advantage for us of war in the East?' asked Eden.

'The German army would be diverted.'

'Oh, but not for long surely? The Russians won't last six weeks, we all know that.'

'Won't they?'

'No. The Red Army is in no fit state to fight a war, Stalin's made sure of that. The officer class has been almost wiped out through the purges since 1937.'

'Wiped out? You're exaggerating surely?'

'No, I don't think so. You only have to look at the figures. Three out of the five marshalls, thirteen out of fifteen army commanders and seventy-five out of the eighty members of the Military Soviet have been shot over the last three years. As have every single commander of every single military district, one hundred and fifty-four out of one hundred and eighty-six divisional commanders, half the brigade commanders and over four hundred out of the four hundred and fifty or so staff colonels.'

'Are you telling us that Stalin has deliberately decapitated his own army?'

'The Red Army is paralysed by fear and political control through the Commissars. No one at any level wants to put their head above the parapet and be shot at.'

'Or just plain shot.'

'Well quite, for taking a decision that might be criticised. And you've only got to look at the Winter War last year to see what poor shape the Red Army's in. Russia sent a million men against a Finnish army of two hundred thousand, and the Finns slaughtered them. The Russians took two hundred and fifty thousand casualties before they started to overwhelm the Finns with sheer weight of numbers. Look back at Spain and the quality of equipment supplied. Hitler and Mussolini helped Franco and Stalin armed the Republicans. Who won there?'

'You make your point.'

'But to make matters worse for them, just think about where the Red Army is today. Russia spent twenty years building fortified defensive lines north and south of the Pripet Marshes in case of a Western invasion. But where's the Red Army now? A hundred miles ahead of them, sitting exposed to the Germans in the occupied zone of Poland while their prepared defences lie empty.'

'What are the chances that Stalin will move the Red Army back?'

'None, in my view. You have to remember that Poland is unfinished personal business for Stalin. He commanded the Red Army that invaded in 1919 which the Poles sent packing.'

'So this is personal?'

'As personal as Stalin gets I'd imagine.'

'Could there be another reason that they are there?'

'Such as?'

'Could Stalin be working up towards an attack on Germany? Stalin's not stupid after all. He'll have read *Mein Kampf* as well. He'll know what Germany really wants and where it's going to turn to next.'

'Possibly, but I seriously doubt it, if for no other reason than going back to 1920 again. Stalin failed leading an army westward in Poland. How happy do you think he would be in having generals that did it successfully today? Always assuming that they could of course and that it didn't just turn into a repeat of Russia's disaster at Tannenberg in 1914.'

'But if it comes to war between them, do we really care who starts it?'

'No, I don't think we do. But what we really need to decide is whether it is in our interests or not.'

'Well it would be a huge diversion of German troops. Even if you accept the Russians won't last six weeks, then the Germans will have still bitten off a huge amount of space to chew on, and Napoleon found out just how big and harsh a place Russia can be. The Germans will need to subdue, garrison and police it. The war itself will interrupt the existing supplies they are receiving from the Soviet Union and it will undoubtedly take quite some time to get these flowing again. So even if the Germans achieve an easy win, then we will have been bought some time, a year, probably more.'

'But in the long term Germany in control of certainly European Russia at least would be more dangerous to us, wouldn't it?'

'In the long run, yes, I think it would as it would have stronger control over a wide range of essential war supplies and could probably make use of an enormous reserve of manpower amongst the non-Russian elements of the current Soviet Union who have no great love for mother Russia.'

'So even having bought some time, in the long run the outcome of such a war is likely to leave us in a worse position with respect to the Germans?'

'Yes, but at least that would be in the long term, as opposed to now when we are facing the imminent prospect of invasion. And a lot of things could change in the long term, there could be other effects.'

'Such as?'

'Well, an increasingly powerful Germany might increase pressure on the US to enter the war. After all, if the Jerries get all the way across Siberia, FDR will be able to see them from Alaska, and they'll link up with the Japs for real.'

'Oh, come on. FDR won't risk being tarred with coming into the war on that basis! The republicans would just accuse him of going to war to save communism, it would be too much of a gift. Don't forget he's got an election coming up in November.'

'Still, whatever the long-term consequences, it is clear that in the short term the impact of the diversion of the German army into an invasion of Russia would be to give us on these islands a breathing space. Is that the common view?'

From around the table there came a murmured general assent.

'So we are all agreed then?' Eden summarised. 'Widening the war is in Britain's interests.'

He nodded to Bruce Lockhart who was making private notes by his side.

'Very well then. So now to the means. I think we'll need a sub group to work on our options so do I have any volunteers? Who would like to start us off?'

Hugh was the first to put up his hand.

*

I had persuaded Libby out for coffee again, and as we sat down the self-same headlines about casualties were facing me in a paper left on the table.

They used to talk about an 'acceptable level of violence' in relation to Northern Ireland when I was a kid. So what was the acceptable level of violence, the acceptable level of deaths in Iraq?

'And for what?' I wondered out loud, showing her the paper before I shoved it aside.

'Makes you wonder how the hell we got into this mess,' she observed.

'That's exactly what our series is going to be about,' I told her.

'Do you know what my Dad called him?' I said casually, to change the subject.

'Who?

'Eden.'

'No?'

'Something along the lines of *the original man with a dodgy dossier*.'

She laughed at that. 'Oooh, I wouldn't bet he was the first.'

'No, I guess not,' I agreed.

'The Zimmerman telegram, The Zinoviev letter. There have been a lot of dodgy dossiers over the years when you think about it,' she continued.

'Sir Tom mentioned the Zinoviev letter when I interviewed him, but not the other one. It rings a vague bell though, but I can't quite place it.'

'It was in World War I.' She seemed surprised that I didn't know more about it, but World War I wasn't really my thing.

'Zimmerman was the German Foreign Secretary and in 1917 they were about to start unrestricted submarine warfare which meant they would inevitably be sinking American ships. So he sent a telegraph to their ambassador in Mexico, telling him that if it looked as though the US was going to enter the war on the Allies' side, he was to offer the Mexicans an alliance and support in recovering Texas, New Mexico and Arizona. We intercepted it, the Admiralty decrypted it in their *Room 40* and then we told the Americans. When it came out in the US Press there was outrage and it was one of the things that helped bring America into the war on our side a month or so later.'

'So if it was real, why call it a dodgy dossier?' I asked.

'Well we had problems in releasing it. Firstly, we had cut their transatlantic cables so the Germans had sent it using the US's own telegraph lines which ran through England, so we didn't want to let the Americans know we were monitoring their diplomatic traffic. And secondly, we didn't want to let the Germans know we could read their codes.'

'So we had to disguise the source?'

'Yes. We pretended we had stolen it from the telegraph office where it was received in Mexico. But the funny thing was, even though it was completely genuine, the Americans were convinced at first it was a forgery. Some in the US Press were only convinced when the Germans admitted it was true.'

'It would fit in well with feeding propaganda into the Press wouldn't it?'

'Yep. And I guess Mr Eden won't have been the last either.'

*

I called Sir Tom again. But he didn't want to speak to me.

'I'm sorry, but I don't think I should give you any further interviews.'

Chapter 6

> It is highly unlikely that an aeroplane, or a fleet of them, could
> ever sink a fleet of Navy vessels under battle conditions.
> FDR, Former Assistant US Secretary of the Navy, 1922

Lieutenant Commander Takeshi Naito, the assistant Japanese naval attaché to Berlin, was woken by an urgent telephone call early in the morning of the 12th November 1940 and by that afternoon he was on a hastily arranged flight from Berlin heading to a rendezvous on the heel of Italy. His resultant report went direct to Admiral Yamamoto, commander of the Imperial Japanese Combined Fleet, and he would be followed in his pilgrimage the following year by a high level Japanese delegation, led by a Rear Admiral and bearing a long list of detailed questions.

*

I needed to put some context around what I was seeing in the files as I worked away at my table in the Registry reading room.

Dusty dry minutes of meetings, *Lt Belvoir (RN) briefed on intelligence received re US appreciation of the situation in the Pacific... the potential for Russo/German conflict was discussed, to be kept under review...* were all very well, but we were going to need the viewers to see, hear and feel the atmosphere of the time they were recorded to breathe some life into them.

So in parallel with my studies in the Registry, I was also brushing up on how the events of the time were unfolding, trying to put aside 20/20 hindsight and seeking to put myself in their shoes, looking to understand how they saw things at the time and what factors played into their considerations.

So when I saw earlier in the same minutes Lt Belvoir had *briefed on the strategic naval priorities in the Mediterranean...* I knew exactly what he would have been referring to.

Operation Judgement.

In late 1940, we were fighting the Italians in the Western desert and their army in Libya needed to be supplied from the mainland. Our forces based in Egypt relied on some supplies coming up through the Suez

Canal, but crucially most arms, munitions and men had to come on convoys, all the way through the Mediterranean from the straits of Gibraltar, where they were at constant risk of attack. So control of the Mediterranean Sea lanes was of critical importance to the war and the battleships of the Italian Fleet, the *Regia Marina*, moored in Taranto harbour on the south coast of Italy posed a major threat to our shipping.

Which is what led to an incredible raid by the Royal Navy's Fleet Air Arm at around midnight on 11 November 1940.

The Fairey Swordfishes were nicknamed Stringbags throughout the Services. As fabric covered biplanes they were completely obsolete in an era of fast metal skinned fighters like Spitfires and ME109s, but they were still the workhorse of the Fleet Air Arm. With the Italian harbour protected by over one hundred anti-aircraft guns and almost two hundred machine guns, losses amongst the slow low flying bombers were expected by Navy planners to run at fifty percent, nevertheless these would go down in history as the twenty-one planes used in the first ever all-aircraft naval attack in history.

For a while it seemed the raid was fated never to happen. To enable the Stringbags to achieve the range required, the aircraft were fitted with an auxiliary fuel tank in place of the third crewman they normally carried, which created an obvious fire hazard. And so it came as little surprise that the whole attack had to be delayed by three weeks after three planes were destroyed by a fire on board one of the carriers.

Then the carrier *HMS Eagle* broke down and so *HMS Illustrious* had to take her aircraft on board to launch the strike on her own.

By this time however the repeated British reconnaissance flights needed as a result of the delays had put the Italian defences on high alert; although without any radar, there was little they could do but wait and ensure they were prepared.

But by that November evening the carrier had steamed into position and the planes were being readied on the crowded deck, armourers setting up half of the planes that night with torpedoes, the others being equipped with bombs and flares.

The normal protection used against the threat of torpedoes in port by every navy were huge nets. Strung out across a harbour, they were designed to catch torpedoes as they ran and prevent them from reaching their targets. But these barriers were heavy and awkward to manoeuvre around an anchorage when ships wanted to move, so sailors found them excessively cumbersome. They could also restrict a ship's ability to rapidly put to sea in the event of a conventional air raid.

And so in shallower waters, like Taranto where the depth on average was only twelve to thirteen fathoms – or about seventy-five feet – since these were thought to be safe from the threat of an air launched torpedo attack, navies tended not to bother to use them.

At about nine o'clock the first wave of twelve aircraft took off into the night from the carrier's deck for the two-hour flight to the target, followed about ninety minutes later by a second wave, with the last plane bringing up the rear on its own after a further twenty minutes' frantic repair work following an earlier taxiing accident on deck.

At just before eleven that evening the harbour at Taranto lit up as the first wave of aircraft attacked, dropping flares to illuminate the target while the first of the bombers struck at the oil tanks of the naval fuel depot.

Then the first flight of three torpedo armed planes swept in low over San Pietro Island at the mouth of the harbour. The lead plane headed straight towards the battleship *Conte di Cavour* and scored a direct hit, blowing a hole almost thirty feet across under her waterline as the battleship's anti-aircraft guns brought the plane down. Jockeying to sweep past the barrage balloons and through a hail of anti-aircraft fire the other two aircraft launched their weapons at the battleship *Andrea Doria* but without success.

Meanwhile the second sub flight of three torpedo armed aircraft in the first wave swept in from the north, hitting the battleship *Littorio* twice, but missing the flagship *Vittorio Vento* with the third, as the other bombers attacked the cruisers and the destroyers in the harbour.

As the first wave of aircraft headed back out to sea the second wave were approaching the scene and at about midnight the harbour was lit up again by the burst of flares, explosions and anti-aircraft fire as they went in. Again the *Littorio* was hit, again the *Vittorio Vento* was narrowly missed, and again one of the aircraft was shot down, but this time one torpedo also hit the battleship *Caio Duilio*, tearing a hole in her side and flooding her forward magazines.

By about twenty to three in the morning the last of the planes had made its way back to land safely on the *Illustrious*.

And so for the loss of two aircraft, with one crew taken prisoner and one crew killed, the Royal Navy had with twenty-one obsolete biplanes, put three modern battleships out of action and destroyed in one night half of the Italian navy's capital ships. The risk of the Regia Marina as a fleet in being and threat to our Mediterranean convoys had effectively been eliminated overnight and the Italian navy subsequently transferred all its ships to Naples.

It had been a triumph of organisation, planning and flying skill. And it was interesting to see in the files that we had been planning how we would take out the Italian fleet at Taranto since 1935, well before the war had started.

We had been prepared.

*

I wasn't surprised to receive a call from Hugh first thing the morning after The Meeting. He wanted to know how long it would take to prepare my report concerning the security of ports on the proposed Far Eastern goodwill tour.

'We need to check on safety for our ships. Can we find out what the Americans are saying about protection at their ports?' he wanted to know.

Not only that. 'While we're at it I think we need to widen it to consider threats to the fleet generally. What about Scapa Flow for example? Can we be sure our ships are safe there?'

'I've signalled a request to the Americans,' I told him, 'but pending hearing from them we're running our own preliminary review as a matter of urgency. I'll bring it over to you as soon as I have it.'

As it turned out, it wouldn't be until the next February that the Americans produced their assessment of the risk.

*

As promised, two days later I knocked on Hugh's office door a little after three bearing the promised report. Given the contents and its importance I had decided to deliver it directly by hand so I could discuss the contents with him, and then return it to the Registry myself.

To my surprise and horror, as I opened the door after his shouted 'Come in' who should be standing beside him studying some papers on a table at the side of the room but Sempill.

'Ah,' Hugh said looking round, 'excellent, is that it?'

'Yes, Sir,' I said, holding it firmly under my arm and carefully not shutting the door behind me. 'But I'm afraid it's Eyes Only and return to Registry after reading.'

'Understood, thank you, Lieutenant,' Hugh said, holding out his hand as he sat down behind his desk.

I stood there, not moving as his hand waited, suspended in mid-air.

'I'm afraid I can't do that, Sir,' I said, eyes fixed on a point somewhere just over his head.

'Ah…'

'Oh, that's alright Hugh,' interrupted Sempill, an amused tone of reasonableness in his voice but a look of pure hatred in his eyes which told me I'd just made an enemy for life, 'The young man is quite right. Security rules are security rules after all.'

He gathered up his papers and pointedly ignoring me, he took his leave of Hugh having agreed to meet again the following day.

'Well I'll leave you to it, ladies,' was his parting shot as he pulled the door closed behind him.

'And now can I see it?' asked Hugh coolly.

I put the file into his hands and stayed standing.

*

Top Secret

Memorandum

Thursday 24th October 1940

As requested, herewith is the Navy's assessment of the risks I requested. As you will see below it makes interesting reading.

Technical Assessment: Risk of aerial torpedo attacks in harbour

As torpedoes dropped from aircraft dive deeply before rising to reach their running depth, aerial torpedo attacks are normally being regarded as impossible in waters with depths of less than 25 fathoms (150 feet). In shallower waters, air launched torpedoes therefore tend to contact the bottom, either burying themselves in the mud, or detonating if they had a chance to arm themselves.

We have been experimenting with a number of methods for the use of torpedoes in shallower waters.

The use of anti-roll stabilisers shows promise but in practise our torpedoes would require substantial development and modification to make this a reliable method.

Given the low speeds of our Fairey Swordfish, we have developed a simpler but effective approach whereby a drum is attached beneath the nose of the aircraft, from which a roll of wire leads to the head of the torpedo. As it is dropped, the tension from the wire pulls up the torpedo's nose, producing a belly-flop rather than a nose dive on entering the sea.

As you can imagine, I have asked the Navy what lessons may be learnt from this research about the protection of our own ships. They seem to be relatively relaxed about any threat to the fleet in Scapa Flow as:

1. *Scapa Flow is generally around seventeen to twenty fathoms (100 to 120 feet) deep and the fleet is of course now extensively protected by torpedo nets, particularly in view of the raid by U47 on 14th October last year which penetrated the anchorage and resulted in the loss of the battleship* Royal Oak *and 810 officers and men.*

2. *Whilst Scapa Flow is within range of German bombers from Norway, these aircraft are not able to fly at the low speeds managed by the Swordfish, would be unprotected by any fighter escort, and Germany has no aircraft carriers that would allow such an escort to be provided.*

With regards to overseas stations and ports which capital ships might visit, the situation varies widely.

HMS Prince of Wales *and HMS* Repulse *should be quite safe from the Japanese while stationed in Singapore for similar reasons to those outlined above as again, the Japanese have no planes with similar low speed capabilities to the Swordfish, and the harbour is well protected with torpedo nets; while the proposed visit to the American fleet for example should be safe as their Hawaii anchorage is only some six to eight fathoms (35 to 50 feet) deep and from what Stephenson's man in the US Navy Department is hearing, the Americans seem equally confident.*

*

As I walked back along the Whitehall corridors to my own office I couldn't help wondering what Hugh and Sempill were up to. The more I thought about it, the less happy I was about giving either of them any information, particularly anything bearing on the Americans or the Japanese. But the truth of it was, I had nothing to go on to back up my feeling of unease. After all, these were senior government advisors, whose sympathies and prejudices were seemingly well known. And what had actually happened after all? Hugh had simply followed up on a request he'd made in the presence of the JIC as chaired by the Foreign Secretary. That was hardly grounds for bandying round accusations in my first month was it?

Not if I wanted to keep my job that is.

Nevertheless, I still remembered my old boss's instruction about keeping my eyes open and his fears that people at surprising levels might be willing to sell us out.

So I decided as I pushed open the door to my own cubby hole, if there was something here and I wanted to do something about it I would need to collect some evidence, which meant I'd need to find a way to get close to Hugh and Sempill, to get involved enough to gather what I need, whilst not too close to become implicated in whatever it was.

To get my hands dirty while staying clean. A tall order.

*

The next day Mr Ginger caught me at reception again as I checked in at Curzon Street, appearing at my elbow and escorting me back to the interview room. His smile was starting to look a bit fixed.

This time it was a stronger warning. I got the distinct impression that it wasn't so much fun for him this time. Perhaps someone had had a word with him.

'So do you just want me to stop talking to Sir Tom? Is that it?' I asked. 'If so, then why don't you just say so?'

'Because we're not worried about you talking to Sir Tom, of course,' he said exasperatedly.

'Why not?' I demanded.

'Because Sir Tom knows what he is doing and would never talk to you about anything that shouldn't be revealed.'

'So it's what I'm trying to talk to Sir Tom about then that's so sensitive is it? But I just don't get it,' I complained, 'Censorship, propaganda, misinformation to the Germans, so what? It was all over sixty years ago.'

'Look, we've given you access to research your programme about diplomacy and the related areas you asked to cover,' he said deliberately, and stabbed the table top with his finger to emphasise his point, 'We're happy to cooperate with you so long as you cooperate with us. All we are asking is that you leave this bit alone.'

He sat back in his chair and gave me what I'm sure he thought was a reassuring smile, 'I don't see how it really fits with what you want to show at all anyway, so just drop it, OK?'

To be honest he was right there. I couldn't see it either, except that it had really piqued my interest. But interest or no interest, I needed their cooperation to do my job and deliver the series.

'OK,' I said. 'OK, I'll drop it.'

'And no bothering Sir Tom?'

'No,' I was surprised at that, 'No *bothering* Sir Tom?' I asked, 'Is that what he said? That I was *bothering* him?'

'I don't know what Sir Tom has said. That sort of thing doesn't filter down to my level you know. But I just think that it's part of what upstairs will be concerned about.' He looked directly at me, 'Particularly now of course.'

'OK,' I said, without thinking to pick up on what he might have meant by 'particularly now'.

'I said I'll drop it and I will.'

'Good.' He stood up and walked me to the door where he called for a commissionaire, 'Thank you.'

*

It turned out I didn't have long to wait. I had a summons to Bruce Lockhart's office the next day and to my utter astonishment, who should be waiting there for me with what turned out to be a proposal but Hugh.

'We're thinking about inviting someone across for a chat,' he said, as we all sat in a set of armchairs around a small table in the corner of the room, 'and we, I, would like your help in making some of the arrangements.'

'Oh, anyone I'd know?' I asked.

'Well you might have heard of him, yes. A chap called Hess.'

'Rudolf Hess?' I stared at him, wondering if he'd gone stark staring mad. 'The Deputy Führer?'

'That's the one,' he nodded calmly. 'Your man Fleming in Naval Intelligence has been reactivating some of the contacts we know of in the pre-war fellow traveller and fifth column organisations, The Link and so on. He's using them as a way to get messages across.'

'What on earth would HMG want to talk to Hess about?' I wondered out loud.

'Oh HMG doesn't,' he told me. 'Officially at least. Let's just say that for the record this is going to be a purely private initiative, certainly as far as Herr Hess would be concerned. Just some influential individuals, people whose voices haven't been properly heard recently, but who are close to power and feel that exploring some kind of accommodation is worth pursuing as a way to resolve the present situation…'

I could see the picture he was painting.

'…you always end up talking to your enemies you know. It's how wars end.'

'But that's treason!' I objected.

'Yes of course it is,' he acknowledged, 'which is why firstly we'd better not get caught and secondly, it's not a real offer.'

'And just what is this fake offer you are intending to make?' I asked.

'Simple. Peace in the West and a free hand in the East.'

'You're going to clear the way for them to attack the Soviet Union?'

'You were at the meeting. Ways and means, ways and means.'

And sitting across the coffee table Bruce Lockhart smiled at me beatifically.

*

'The Service has form on dodgy dossiers doesn't it, son?'

It was a great help being able to stay with the folks when I was down. If I'd had to pay for digs as well while I was in London to research the files I knew I would have quickly been in dire straits. Besides which, Dad was also being his usual supportive and generous self, helping out with subs of cash here and there. The gee-gees had obviously done well recently.

I took my cup of hot water, having wafted an Earl Grey teabag gently in its general direction, upstairs to where I'd set up my laptop so I could check my emails.

It was very much the usual.

Viagra. Delete.

Viagra. Delete.

Cialis. What was Cialis I wondered? At least I'd heard of Viagra. Delete.

Did I want to make girls gasp? Well that depends, I thought. Delete.

An 'important notice from HSBC Bark' asking me to verify my online account details which was a bit difficult since I didn't bank with them. Delete.

'Did I know that girls in my area were just dying to meet me?' Well I doubted it, thank you. Delete.

An 'urgent request for your kind assistance' as someone who had been recommended to the sender as a suitable person to help them out with transferring US$26m from dormant accounts in Nigeria into my account.

I felt like putting them in touch with HSBC Bark. Delete.

'At last, proof that Iraq did have WMD.'

Hello, what's this? I wondered, as I opened it and the attached picture loaded up. Now this at least was from a mate.

It was very well done. A photo of a spoof till receipt from US Government, signed by Bush senior, for delivery of a consignment of gas and nukes.

'Dad'll love this,' I thought switching on the printer to run off a copy, 'and so will Libby'.

*

'So how's it going?' Mum asked, sipping from her mug of tea the next morning.

'Oh, alright I think, thanks. I was telling Dad all about it yesterday.'

'Well you know your Father,' she protested, 'he never tells me anything.'

'Now, Mother,' Dad said from over by the sink where he was washing up, 'that's just not true.'

'Oh yes it is,' she retorted, 'You know as well as I do that this whole family operates on a need to know principle.'

She switched back to me, ignoring the amused snort of feigned protest from behind her.

'Are you off up to London again?' she asked.

'Yes.'

'Oh, and here,' she called as I headed for the door, 'before I forget again. There was a letter came for you yesterday. It's on top of the cupboard in the hallway.'

'Thanks,' I said, and just remembered to grab it on my way out as I pulled on my coat for the walk up to the station.

It was strange that something had come to me down here in Surrey rather than at home, I thought, as I walked briskly past the rows of neat Victorian villas and terraced houses that lay behind the High Street full of coffee shops and estate agents. I was travelling into town later than the main commuter rush so there would be plenty of seats. I was also my father's son and as usual I had allowed myself loads of extra time so I'd have a while to kill at the station before the train was due.

Plenty of time to grab myself a coffee and a paper from the stall at the station and have a quick scan through whatever was in the letter.

*

I had smuggled the piece of paper into the reading room folded inside the pad I brought to take notes on.

I waited until mid-morning and I was ready for a coffee before I sneaked it into the front of the file I was reading while Libby was over at her desk.

'Hey look what I have here!' I said.

'What's that?' she said looking up from where she had been reading.

'Come and see,' I said, staring intently at the file in front of me as I heard the scrape of her chair.

'What is it?' she said, leaning over my shoulder, 'what have you found?'

I handed her the print out. 'You might want to pass it on.'

'Well ha-ha,' she said deliberately, with a smile playing around her mouth as she read it, 'Yes, very funny.

'You might however,' she continued, proffering the print back to me between the tips of her outstretched fingers, 'want to keep that to yourself. I suspect it's a bit of a sore subject around here.'

'No sense of humour in the Service?'

'Oh, plenty, I think. It's just that given what's been going on in that department, do you really want to test it right now?'

'Well no I guess not,' I conceded.

'Well then.'

'Coffee?' I asked, as she turned away.

'No thanks,' she said, 'not today.'

*

The ginger haired guy was waiting for me at reception yet again as I handed back my chit for my jacket and bag that afternoon.

'Hi there. Leaving early today? Could you step in here again, I just wanted a quick word if I may? It won't take a minute.'

'Why yes, fine, I said. I've got a little while, I'm just meeting someone.'

Back outside a few minutes later I was glad he hadn't asked me any more questions about that, since the truth was that I wouldn't have known the answers.

I walked down to Piccadilly and Green Park tube.

I had a rendezvous, at somewhere close to Paddington station.

Chapter 7

> ...alongside our values of courage, respect and integrity, we
> place a premium on creativity... We will never prevail through
> scale or force of numbers. It is creativity, innovation and sheer
> guile that give us the edge.
>
> Alex Younger, C, Chief of the Secret Intelligence Service,
> writing to
> *The Economist*, 30 September 2017

Now I was here in this squalid little hotel.

I had been wondering if I would recognise who was speaking. See if it was someone I knew playing a trick on me. One of the guys from the office, for example. People knew about the series and it wasn't beyond some of them to want to wind me up. *Hey why don't we pull his leg? He's off seeing the spooks, let's set him up on some secret squirrel stuff. It'll be a laugh.*

I shouldn't have bothered. It was a man's voice, but that was about all I could tell. The sound had a metallic quality to it. He was obviously using some kind of device to disguise it. If I had to pick him out in a line up on the basis of what I was hearing, I'd probably have to go for a Dalek if they had one there.

'Well here I am. I came. So who are you and what do you want?' I asked.

'Me? Oh, that's simple. I want you to prove yourself,' said the voice.

'Prove myself? What do you mean prove myself? What for?'

'I need to see what you can do before I give you the keys to the castle.'

'What on earth are you talking about?' I demanded. 'What keys? What castle?'

'Look. How much do you really want to know about deception?' he said, suddenly throwing me off balance.

'What is there to know?' I asked casually.

'More than you can possibly imagine, despite what you've found already. You've only scratched the surface,' he said. 'Look, let me try again. How much do you know about World War II?'

'Some,' I shrugged to myself.

'And how much about it do you think is still being kept secret by the Government?'

'Some bits, I guess.'

'You guess, or you know?'

'OK then, I guess,' I answered. I was here now, I thought. I might as well play along for a bit and find out what he was after. 'They had been keeping Bletchley Park quiet. There's certainly a number of mysteries still, Hess and stuff that no one has really explained.'

'Well they won't have. The Hess files are sealed until 2016,' he said, which was interesting as I knew he was correct.

'I really don't understand why not,' I said. 'It just gives the conspiracy theorists more things to work around.'

'Well if you knew what was in them you would know why they're not being released.'

'And you do?' I asked.

'Yes,' he said with an air of certainty.

I couldn't resist that. 'So what is in them?'

'I'm not telling you that!'

'What are you going to tell me then?' I asked, 'Why get me here? Is it just to play games?'

He didn't seem phased at all. 'All in good time.'

'Look, this isn't getting us very far is it then? Dark hints about some conspiracy? Is that what this is all about?'

He sounded amused at my irritation, 'And you're not interested in conspiracies?'

'No. I'm a cock-up man myself,' I said flatly, 'Like I keep telling my Dad, the world's too complicated a place to pull a few levers in secret and have everything work out the way you want it to.'

'It seems a bit odd to be researching deception then if you don't believe in conspiracies,' he observed, 'Surely that's just what deceptions are all about?'

He had a point, I thought.

'Look, Mr X or whoever you are,' I said, 'I'm a researcher, I read the files for a living. I know that you never uncover all the facts. You get enough to tell the story and then you move on. And real life is messy, there are always bits that don't quite tie up, missing bits of information, loose ends, conflicting statements, things that could be interpreted one way or the other. Just because something is odd or not completely explained doesn't mean that there's some big secret behind it.'

'But then that's the thing about secrets isn't it?' he retorted, 'As dear old Donald put it, *unknown unknown* and all that. For all the flak he'd had about it, that sometimes you don't know, what you don't know, is a very old idea.'

'I know, or yes I guess then, that we don't know everything,' I admitted. 'Some are just things that aren't known, and I guess there are some things that the government still doesn't want us to know about, although with everything that's come out since the war you would guess we had aired most of our dirty linen by now. Yalta and carving up Europe with Stalin. Sending the Russian Cossacks back to him to be slaughtered. The bombing of Dresden.'

'Those are the knowns,' he said, 'But then what about the *unknown unknowns*?'

'But how do you know there are any *unknown unknowns* as you put it? How does anybody?' I protested.

'Well maybe they are known to me.'

I didn't answer.

'All right,' he continued, 'let's just say for argument's sake that I am right for a moment and there are still secrets. Secrets that the Government does not want you to know. Why do you think that might be? Do you think anything from World War II could be relevant to what's going on today?'

Sat on the bed in the dingy room I shrugged, 'Not much I guess. It's been the best part of what, sixty-five years or so since it started? How much relevance could any secret still have?'

'Well if it's still a secret, that answers your question doesn't it?' he said.

I was puzzled. 'Does it? Why?'

'Think about it,' he said, 'Because the only reasons for keeping something a secret is because either it is still valuable, or it is still damaging or even dangerous. Why else would you go to the time and trouble to keep it secret?'

Well yes, why else indeed, I thought.

'You have to appreciate that the things I can tell you could bring down the government and cause the mother of all international incidents,' he continued.

'What? That's a bit dramatic isn't it?'

'Maybe it is, but all the same, I'm perfectly serious. And perfectly sane too if that's what you are wondering.'

Well it had crossed my mind. 'But seriously, you can't expect me to believe that?'

'We'll see,' he said calmly, 'Still, that's just the things I can tell you. Whether I will or not is an entirely different matter.'

'So why tell me at all?'

'So that you appreciate the seriousness of what we are doing here, talking like this. Why we have to take serious precautions, and why we have to take precautions seriously.'

He paused to emphasise his point.

'The things I can tell you have huge ramifications. They have implications for national security and they have implications for HMG's place in the world.'

He was obviously Civil Service I had concluded early on in our conversation, just from the way he spoke, the language he used. I had heard it before. Quite high up I would guess from the way he was talking, if he was genuine of course. But that was a big if, and I was, I reminded myself, a card carrying suspicious, jaded and cynical hack who still had the real fear that I was just being pissed about by some time-wasting nutcase.

'So why do you want to tell me then?' I challenged, 'Do you want to set the record straight? Is that it?'

He sounded amused, 'What's the harm in that?'

'What's the harm indeed?'

'It's only right that people should know what has been done in their name and why.'

'Know what?'

'What I can tell you.'

I had lost patience to a degree by this stage, 'Oh come on, stop fencing for God's sake. If you're going to talk then talk or we're just wasting our time here. Such as?'

'Well, since you raised it, Hess, for example.'

Oh God, I groaned to myself, not Hess. I should have known. There's been more conspiracy crap written about Hess and his flight to England in May 1941 than about almost anything else. I'm just surprised nobody's had him at the grassy knoll yet.

'What about him?'

'Hess is interesting. And yes, before you say it, there is a lot of nonsense written about him. But Hess was very much the ideological brains behind the Nazis, certainly at the start. People always think of him as Hitler's secretary in prison but the truth is he wrote most of *Mein Kampf* for Hitler, it's mostly his ideology. Hitler was a German nationalist to begin with, it was Hess who led him down the path of Aryan racial supremacy. Hitler had always admired England and the English fighting man from his days in the trenches in World War I, and from how he saw we ran our empire around the world. He wanted us as allies, not enemies. At least he did until we thwarted him. But for Hess it was purer than that. For Hess we were Aryan blood brothers, destined to stand together against other races.'

'You were talking to the Germans?' I guessed.

'Oh yes,' he confirmed quite calmly, 'You always maintain links in any war. Wars always end and the best and quickest way to progress getting to an endpoint is by talking. Historically, demanding absolute unconditional surrender the way we did of the Germans is very unusual. Most wars end at peace talks, so whoever you are fighting you always try to keep some channels open somewhere. You always talk. You only have to look at Gerry Adams today.'

'Prove it to me.'

'Keep on going and I will.' He paused, 'Whatever you think now, I'm perfectly serious you know. I will show you that I mean what I say and then I will call you again.'

'Prove it to me then,' I challenged again, 'any nutter can talk about conspiracies and hidden evidence. What I need to see is real.'

'Oh certainly. That's what I want you to see. Now you're looking at Admiral Godfrey's boys in Naval Intelligence at the moment.'

I sat bolt upright on the bed in shock. Now how the hell did he, whoever the hell he was, know that? I had only got them out this week. Naval Intelligence files were a must see since Ian Fleming had headed up NID17, the part that came up with schemes and coordinated strategy with the other Intelligence Services.

'Well then. I will give you a tip.'

'A tip?'

'A pointer. The first part of a jigsaw if you like.'

'All right. But I hope I'm not going to be wasting my time,' I said, 'What is it?'

'You've been reading about Taranto,' he said which scared me again. Just how the hell did he know this stuff?

'Have a look at the Service's files on Operation Judgement. Don't bother with the Navy's operational ones, it's the Service's assessments that you want to read. Just see if you find anything odd, anything inconsistent in those files. Then we'll talk again.'

'But how?'

*

'So how did it go today then?' Dad asked as he put the kettle on. Like I've said, it was an automatic reaction in our house as soon as anyone walked in through the door. There was an assumption that nothing ever happened without the need for a cup of tea to be brewed.

'Oh, all right I suppose,' I said, dropping my bag on the kitchen table, 'I got called in again for another of their little friendly chats though.'

'A chat, what about?'

'Oh, on whether I was still digging where they didn't want me to, or had given up?'

'So what did you say?'

'Well it's a bit difficult to tell isn't it, when they won't tell me where not to dig? But I did say that I wasn't talking to anyone; that they could speak to Sir Tom if they didn't believe me.'

'Why Sir Tom?'

'Because I'm sure he was the one who had set them on to me. I tried to get them to confirm it but they wouldn't of course.'

'And what did they say to that?'

'That there was no need. That I was free to carry on of course.'

'So that was that?'

'Apparently so.'

'But it wasn't just a chat was it?'

'No, of course it wasn't.'

'Is it a second warning?'

'I guess so,' or a third, I thought to myself.

'Is there something they know?'

'I don't know,' I said truthfully. Since I really don't know myself. And what's more I couldn't find out. My man, or Mr X as I called him, had been very specific that this was to be a one-way street. At least until he decided otherwise.

He would text me a message to my mobile. He wasn't worried about security too much on that and I wouldn't recognise the number as he would be using pre-paid mobiles that he would ditch regularly although he would also send me other, more general messages as well, so that the meetings did not stand out. Traffic he called it. So the real messages would look perfectly innocent, just giving a time by which I had to be somewhere to meet up for a drink. But each time we spoke on the phone, he would tell me where the next 'meeting' was to be and also how many hours I would have to add to, or take off, the time in his next message to know when actually to be there.

'Hotels?' I had asked.

'Mainly.'

'And what if I miss a meeting?'

The fall back was to be at the same location an hour later the following day and an hour later again the next day. After that he would have to decide how he contacted me again.

'Look. Is this all really necessary?'

'Yes,' he said firmly, 'I cannot afford to compromise my security. You will understand why when you see what I want you to read.'

'You've got something for me to read?'

'Yes.'

'Where is it?' I had asked, looking around the room.

'Oh it's not there, if that's what you're thinking.'

'So where is it?'

'Don't worry. You'll get it soon enough,' he had said, and then he hung up.

*

Mum was excited when she saw me appear downstairs. 'Did Father tell you? There was a call for you yesterday.'

No, he hadn't as it happened. I hadn't spoken to him yet. Although since Dad was standing just over the other side of the kitchen you did wonder why she hadn't asked him before I came downstairs.

It had been a call from an American agent, she told me.

'Your Father took the details,' she said, as Dad reached for the pad of old envelopes held together with a treasury tag that always hung by the telephone as a makeshift note pad. 'It sounds very interesting, she continued, 'they want to talk to you about your project. They want to know how you are getting on.'

'They said something about inviting you to go over to the US to talk about it,' chimed in Dad.

'Who's paying?' I asked.

'They are, he said.'

Mum was right, this was potentially a very interesting development, 'Did they say why?'

'Why they were interested?'

'Yes.'

'He said there was a big interest in the US in anything to do with British Intelligence. Le Carré, Philby, all that sort of thing.'

'A big interest?' I asked, sounding a note of surprise.

'Well then not big perhaps,' Dad conceded, 'but dedicated.'

'That's good isn't it?' chipped in Mum from over her cup of tea.

'Still,' Dad said, 'it seems a bit strange that they called here doesn't it? How would they know you were here? Why wouldn't they have called the Beeb instead? And how would an American agent know what you were working on anyway?'

The same questions had been going through my mind as well. 'Perhaps my agent's being efficient at marketing my work?' I suggested, as I walked over to Dad to take the scrap of paper with the caller's details on it.

Would be nice, I thought, but didn't say out loud.

'I'll give this guy a bell later on.'

*

There were quite a few files listed in the Registry on Taranto, but there were two main ones that seemed as though they fell into the category of assessment that Mr X had suggested. I made sure I ordered them separately over two succeeding days.

As I didn't really know what I was looking for I took extensive notes on the first file, just to make sure that I had enough to check the second against to see if I could spot an inconsistency. But as it turned out I really hadn't needed to bother. Because the two files were just about the same in every respect but one. Their conclusions, which were diametrically opposite.

But why produce two versions of the same report with completely opposite findings? I asked myself.

It was a puzzle. But it did prove one thing. Mr X whoever he was, obviously did know what he was talking about. Inconsistencies. Mind you, I had decided that Mr X was serious long before I had worked my way through to the end of the second file on Operation Judgement.

I had made up my mind almost instantaneously in fact, just after I'd turned over the third page in the first file I'd requested and found 'it'.

It was clearly wrong.

Wrong in the sense of not belonging.

And probably also wrong, I guessed, without even touching it, in the sense of being a breach of Section 1, subsection 2, of the Official Secrets Act 1920, carrying as I knew from the lecture they had given me as I had signed the documentation to obtain my research authorisation, a potential penalty on conviction on indictment of imprisonment for a term not exceeding two years, or a fine, or both.

I looked up but there was no one else in the room other than Libby and she was working at her desk over by the door. I glanced down again at the file I had half opened on the table and quietly turned the second page over again.

In contrast to the yellowing faded pages of old Civil Service foolscap I was used to seeing in file after file, the sheets that had been slipped into the folder were shockingly modern and ordinary white pieces of A4 photocopier paper, folded in half.

Casually, and keeping the front of the file lifted up so that neither Libby nor anyone who might come in could see what I was looking at I slipped the pages open and scanned the contents.

It was a photocopy, over two sheets. The original had obviously been typed and had still been in its file when the document had been put on the copier. You could see the treasury tags that held the pages together and the top right of the first sheet had the distortion and black edging that came from not having been pressed down on the platen properly. A job by someone in a hurry I wondered?

It was the text of a speech. A relatively short one.

It was dated Monday 21 October 1940 but I had never heard of it before. I guess that outside of the higher echelons of the Services very few had by the look of it. It had been made to a very select group of people, at the launch of a new committee, so on the face of it that wasn't so surprising. But what was interesting was the speaker.

Member of Parliament.

The First Lord of the Treasury.

Prime Minister.

The Right Honourable Winston Spencer Churchill.

Was there something significant about the date I wondered? I thought about what I knew about the situation at the time. It was after the Battle of Britain, and it was after Hitler had postponed Sealion, as Churchill would have known through the Ultra transcripts of the Enigma intercepts, but otherwise I couldn't think of anything. The date meant nothing to me.

But the real kicker was the audience. The Press Commission.

The bloody Press Commission? I thought to myself as I looked at it. Lieutenant T Belvoir would have been at that meeting. And the speech seemed to have absolutely nothing to do with the Press at all.

I needed to speak to Sir Tom again. But I knew I couldn't. He simply wouldn't return my calls these days.

What I had instead was my very own Deep Throat, my Mr X.

But only as and when he called me.

*

As for the second piece of paper, well it was shocking in a number of ways.

Again it was a photocopy, this time of an extract from a manuscript, a book by the look of it which had been submitted for clearance by the Service.

And the author of this work? Oh, that was the best bit, that was the bloody killer. One Commander Sir Tom Belvoir DSO Royal Navy (Retired).

He'd only written a sodding book.

> So gentlemen, if I may summarise what seem to be our conclusions.

> Firstly, to be able to survive in the longer term and then to

prevail in the struggle ahead, we need the United States to enter the war. However, at the moment, despite the understanding at some higher levels that this is in their long-term interests, due to popular sentiment there is no realistic prospect of this occurring unless there is a significant change in circumstances.

So our focus needs to be survival in the short and medium term until such time as this may change. Are we agreed?

There was a general murmur of consent and in some cases a reluctant nodding of heads around the table.

Secondly, in the event of an outbreak of war between Germany and the Soviet Union, whilst we consider it is likely to result in a rapid German victory on the field of battle, whether they ultimately win or not, such an action is also likely to tie Germany up for a considerable period in dealing with and consolidating its control of large newly conquered territories.

Thus, while in the longer term it is likely to be highly disadvantageous as it removes a threat to Germany's rear, in the short term it may give us a breathing space as a significant distraction and diversion of its forces.

Eden looked up and scanned the room. Again, are we agreed gentlemen?

There was no major dissention and he took the silence as consent.

So then, given our short-term priorities, the policy of HMG needs to be that the outbreak of war between Germany and the Soviet Union is in the best interests of the British Empire and all steps which can be taken to achieve this objective should be considered by this committee?

The minutes recorded this as carried *nem com.*

The note on the file instructed the section was to be redacted in the interests of national security if any publication of the book were to be authorised.

Jesus! I sat back in my chair, shocked to my core. I mean, I wasn't naïve, I suppose deep down I'd have always guessed this sort of discussion went on at top level. These were statesmen playing diplomacy for real after all.

But to read it in black and white, the brutal cynicism of the pure national interest, its undeniable cold logic untrammelled by considerations of rights or wrongs or the consequences for others. That was shocking.

Our Government had taken a decision that it was in our national interest to promote the outbreak of a war in which tens of millions of people would eventually be killed.

And Sir Tom had sat in at that meeting, I thought, as I slipped the photocopied pages between the sheets of my pad of paper.

Chapter 8

For any nation, the right history is worth 100 Divisions.

Adolf Hitler

As it happened I didn't have long to wait. Which by now didn't come as much of a surprise.

The hotel this time was off Baker Street. We were obviously going a little more up market for our chats, I thought, as the telephone in the room went and the receptionist announced that she had a call to put through to me.

There weren't any pleasantries. He didn't actually say *EXTERMINATE*, but it sounded close.

'You saw the speech?' It was rhetorical rather than interrogative. 'You understand its significance?'

'Christ yes,' I said, 'Is that for real? It's a mandate to do anything.'

'Yes, it's real enough,' he confirmed flatly, 'or at least a photocopy of something that's real enough, although I doubt that you'll ever get to see the original. But really, it's not such a shock is it? Remember, Churchill would do anything,' he said, 'Gallipoli, Zeebrugge, SOE. Winston always liked the unorthodox stroke.'

'Winston?' I was surprised by the familiarity in his tone of voice, 'Did you know him?'

'That's not particularly relevant, is it now?'

'I don't know, do I?' I said pointedly. 'I don't know a whole hell of a lot just now, not about you, not about what you've got me looking at or what sort of game you are playing.'

'No, you don't,' he said, 'and I'm afraid that's the way it's going to stay until I think it's safe to be otherwise.'

'So what if I don't want to play your game?' I challenged

'Well I don't think that's very likely is it?' he asked.

'At least for the moment. You've been picked as lead researcher on what's supposed to be a landmark programme,' he said, showing once again that he knew far more about me and what I was doing than I felt comfortable with, 'and you need this to be a success don't you? You need this to be your springboard into what you really want to be. This is your chance of a breakthrough and you have to make it work, don't you?'

And the thing was, he was right. It was true. All of it.

'So I think you'll be keen to do anything, anything within reason that is, to make it a success. After all I've just shown you something that you would never have got to see in a million years, and I've started you off down the track to something absolutely astonishing.'

'So you say.'

'Yes, so I say. But you've seen what I can do. So now you have a choice, don't you?' he continued remorselessly, 'You can stick with me and go where I want to take you, see what I want to show you; or you can go off on your own to research this series and see where that can get you. But then you'll just be following the files that are open to everybody who's looking, and working without anyone who can point you in the right direction.'

'And?'

'And my bet is that you'll choose to stick with me. You'll want to see what it is I have. You'll take the chance that I might really mean what I say; that I can lead you where no one else has gone, show you what no one else has seen, and deliver you something truly earth shattering for your programmes. Something that will really make you.'

'Because you know where the bodies are buried? Is that it?'

There was a moment's silence on the other end of the line. 'Something like that I suppose,' said the Dalek voice eventually. 'So what about it? Are you interested or not in what I have to tell you?'

'Yeah,' I said, submitting as he obviously had known I would. I really couldn't walk away from this, and what secrets he might be in a position to divulge now, but even so, I was still concerned, 'but slipping me copies of classified documents from inside the Registry could also get me sent down you know. There's still such a thing as the Official Secrets Act.'

'Oh, I know all about the Official Secrets Act. I signed my copy before you were born.'

He changed the subject.

'Anyway, you saw the files?' Again, it wasn't a question. He obviously knew I had seen the files on Taranto, otherwise how would I have seen the copy of the speech that he had put, or had had put I supposed, into one of them for me to find. This was someone with high level access. It had to be.

'Yes.'

'And again, do you understand the significance?'

'Well yes, I see the issue,' I said confidently, 'I could see the inconsistency.'

Whether I understood the significance was nowhere near as clear.

'What I don't understand is why there are two files?' I asked, 'There are two reports, they have almost exactly the same information in them, but I don't understand why they have diametrically opposite conclusions.'

It was true. I had read and reread the second file in growing confusion. The text matched completely to the notes I had made on the first file, except where it came to discussing some of the technical details of how the attack had been achieved in much shallower water than was normally thought possible at the time for torpedoes and what that meant, if anything, for the vulnerability of our fleet at anchor in Scapa Flow and ships visiting foreign stations. In one version they were safe, in the other they weren't. It was as simple as that.

'Why indeed?' the Dalek sounded amused. I guessed I had just passed some kind of test.

'So what would anyone want those for?' I continued, 'They can't both be right?'

'Well,' he said, 'just think about it for a moment. What do you think you can you do with reports that conclude the answers are Yes and No respectively?'

As he said it, of course the answer was obvious. To be able to prove whatever you wanted to prove. And that also answered the question as to why these would be in the Service's files? Why it hadn't just been a navy matter.

'Maybe you needed to have the right story get out.'

'That's right.'

'But there's one thing I don't understand,' I asked, 'which is the right story?'

'The one that suited our needs at the time of course.'

I thought I saw what he was driving at now. 'What, disinformation? To protect the fleet? To be able to leak it to the Germans that we've looked at the dangers of that type of attack at Scapa Flow and it won't work against us, so we're safe?'

'It might put them off thinking about trying something like that themselves mightn't it?' he said.

'Yes, it might,' I agreed, 'or it might just make them think we're being complacent and taking too few precautions, so that it's something worth looking at?'

'And what would happen if you deliberately leaked the version that says we are vulnerable at Scapa Flow to the Germans?' he challenged. 'What would the result of that be do you think?'

'Christ almighty!' I was genuinely shocked. 'No one in their right mind would have dared do that surely at the time? To risk luring the Germans in to attack the fleet at its base? Surely you'd be shot for suggesting something like that.'

'Unless of course,' he answered, 'that you leaked it in such a way that you calculate they will think it's a double bluff...'

'That we were setting a trap?'

'If you like. That if we have that report, not only will we have taken action to protect our battleships, which we had anyway with torpedo nets, but that we will also be ready and waiting for their bombers if they come. There would be no fighter escort that far from Norway don't forget, and the Germans had already had a bloody nose in trying to bomb the North East. In short that we had set a trap to destroy the *Luftwaffe* in Norway.'

'Christ. Using the fleet as bait?'

'This is all hypothetical of course.'

Jesus, I thought, my head reeling. Once you peered over the edge into a world of infinitely receding *if they know – that we know – that they knows,* you had to cling onto the edge before you started to spiral away. How the hell did you keep a grip on sanity and even reality once you started down the path of deception at this scale and complexity, I wondered?

*

I needed to talk to someone.

And, if she would agree to talk, Libby was really the only one I could bounce ideas off. She had clearance and knew what was in the files I was looking at.

So, the next day in the reading room I told her it would be useful just to be able to talk to her in that way, to help me get my thoughts in order.

'You don't mind, do you?' I asked. 'It won't compromise what you do?'

'I wouldn't have thought so,' she said, after a moment's consideration. 'Obviously I can't speak on behalf of the Service.'

Which led to a thought that had been worrying at me for a little while now.

'Do you mind me asking you something else too?'

She smiled, 'Depends what it is, doesn't it?'

'Do you have to report on me? What I'm looking at I mean, what I'm asking about and so on?'

'Oh yes, in a way. Don't worry,' she added, I guess seeing my face fall, 'I'm not here to spy on you but there's a paper trail obviously in terms of what files you are asking for, which you get to see, which you don't and I have to fill out a daily log about any supplementary questions that you want answered.'

'Oh, OK,' I said, a bit uncertainly, I suppose that made sense. After all the Service weren't just going to let anyone have the free run of the files, and it was part of the Civil Service as well. The idea of a paper trail and a log of requests and files seen should hardly have come as a surprise.

'So what sort of thing did you want to talk about?' she asked.

'Well if it's OK by you, I'd like to run some things past you.'

And we talked, for an hour or so I guess, with me telling her about the files and what I was seeing, her questions helping me to shape in my mind how things were coming together for the book. Eventually of course the subject of Hess came up.

'The surrender theories?' she asked acutely. 'Is that one of the things you want to look at? Isn't that a bit off the serious track you are supposed to be on?'

'Well, there have been conspiracy stories before,' I said, 'You ought to hear my Dad.'

*

'The idea of talking to Hess about peace, I mean really talking to him, isn't as farfetched as it sounds,' said Dad reflectively that evening.

'There were peace talks and contacts with elements in Germany going on throughout the war, and even before it. You had German officers and diplomats sending us messages in '38 and '39 that we needed to stand up to Hitler. Even discounting Hess, you still had other high-ranking Nazis starting talks during the war, Von Papen for example. Even Himmler sent out feelers about a negotiated peace settlement with the Western powers in 1943 through his Finnish masseur Kersten and contacts in Sweden, for God's sake.

'Don't forget,' he continued, 'that the Russians were always opposed to releasing Hess right to the bitter end, even after he was the last man left in Spandau, however much the British and Americans suggested that they should. In some ways it would seem strange that the Russians still had such a vendetta about Hess of all people after all that time. After all he was already in custody here before Hitler even attacked the Soviet Union.'

'But that's rather the point isn't it?' I said. 'There was always the theory that the Russians blamed him. After all he was really only trying for peace with Britain so that Germany had its back covered for their attack on the Soviet Union.'

But then there was also the theory I knew that we had been feeding Hess the line that we were holding on in the hope that Russia would come to our aid, which was pretty much what Hitler thought we thought anyway. So that part of the reason for attacking Russia was to take away our hope of rescue from that quarter so we would then give up.

'Well I doubt the files will ever prove it one way or the other by the time they're actually released.'

'Do you think that's what they are worried about you having got too close to?' Dad asked. 'To Hess and the truth about some kind of peace talks? Perhaps even a deal?'

I was dismissive of that as an idea. The subject of Hess was no biggie as I saw it, whatever the truth was, not these days. As I'd told Libby, there had been enough conspiracy theories, rumours and allegations around for years about him.

That we had been talking to him and the peace negotiations were serious.

That we hadn't been talking to him and he was just a nut case.

That we had been and it was just a stalling operation to buy us time.

That we hadn't realised it was Hess that we were actually dealing with in our talks until he had missed his landing strip and bailed out over Scotland.

That through our embassy in Switzerland we had bought a pair of drop tanks for the type of ME110 that Hess flew in which would have given it enough fuel capacity to make the return flight to Germany if he had managed to land as planned.

You paid your money and you took your choice.

'Or possibly more than one of them at once?'

'What do you mean?'

'Well you know what secret services are like. Little rival empires, competing organisations, bureaucratic infighting and empire building. What if some were really talking to the Nazis and some were only pretending to talk? Might that be what they were trying to cover up?'

'Are you serious?' I hadn't thought about that.

'What, the left hand not knowing what the right hand was doing?'

'Yes.'

He shrugged. 'Well of course. It happens all the time. It's just the nature of the beast.'

*

'You do realise that it's all a distraction, don't you?' Dad asked across the table, continuing his interrogation the next morning without missing a beat.

'What?'

'Your chums over at MI5 and MI6.'

'Why do you say that?' I protested.

'Well just think about it. You, and everybody else, are always interested in what MI5 and MI6 get up to.'

'So?' I tore another croissant into jammable chunks.

'So, you completely fail to look at where the real secret stuff is going on.'

'Which is?'

'Well,' he leant across conspiratorially, 'I can't say too much, but haven't you ever wondered whatever happened to MI1, MI2, MI3 and MI4?'

I laughed, 'Ah it all becomes clear to me now.'

'Well,' he said, sitting back in his chair, 'don't say I didn't give you a lead.'

Just then Mother wandered back in from the hallway where she'd been picking up the post. 'What's going on?' she asked.

'Oh,' I said, looking up, 'nothing, it's just Father winding me up again.'

She laughed and clapped her hand on my shoulder. 'Ah well dear, there's nothing new there. He's been doing it to me for the best part of fifty years.'

Father smiled and stuck his tongue out at her. 'Now then Mother, just you get on with making that cup of tea and let him finish his breakfast.'

'Are you up to London again?'

'Yes.'

And I was, but not to Curzon Street. I had yet another appointment. In yet another hotel. And hopefully today was the day I got to meet Mr X, my Deep Throat.

*

I put down the paper I was reading as he came into the room. I suppose it shouldn't really have come as a surprise. But it did.

'I thought you didn't want to talk to me?' I asked Sir Tom, as he sat across the room from me in the hotel suite he'd hired. This was a bright and comfortable room, I noticed. He obviously didn't fancy slumming it himself for a meet.

'That was deliberate,' he said calmly. 'I wanted to ensure that I was not thought to be talking to you. And to be honest, I wanted to see how far you would go before I let you know who I was.'

'So I've passed some kind of test, have I?'

'Yes. I should think so.'

'Well thank you very much,' I said, with more than a hint of sarcasm in my voice, 'I hope that it's going to have been worth it. So let's hear what you have to say.'

'I think you'll find eventually that it has. But first, before I give you more, I think I need you to talk, I need to know what you have and how far you have got so far.'

'This is silly isn't it? You've obviously got your sources within the Service; otherwise how did you get that speech in that file for me to see?'

He waved that one away with a smile.

'No. It's not just what you've seen, even if I knew all that; which I don't by the way,' he said, emphasising the point.

Whether I believed him or not was another question.

'But it's what you have made of what you've seen that's important. Intelligence work is about more than just gathering information, it's not just about capabilities you know. It's about interpretation and assessment and most crucially it's about intentions.'

He looked at me as though trying to judge that I knew what he meant.

'Look, for example, it wasn't enough in 1990 to know that Saddam had an army of a million men. Everyone in government and the Services knew it was ten times the size of ours, he had five thousand tanks and more attack helicopters alone than the RAF had aircraft in total. The problem wasn't knowing that he had the capability to do something, that was obvious, and more to the point, was also reasonably easy to find out from satellite photos and similar sorts of technical sources. No, the problem was working out what he was planning to do with them. His intentions.'

'Which we didn't until afterwards.'

He nodded, 'Which we didn't until he rolled into Kuwait. Because it can actually be quite difficult to do. How can you tell what's really going on in a man's head?'

I wasn't going to be dragged into that sort of discussion. We could be here forever with something like that, so I decided to ensure we kept to the point, whatever that was actually going to be of course. 'And we paid the price for it.'

'Yes,' he said, a sudden sad tone in his voice breaking through for a moment that I hadn't heard previously, before it snapped back under control, 'and as you say, we paid the price for it. So, now I need to know how far you think you have worked things through.'

So I told him what I knew and what I thought. Which didn't really amount to much more than loose ends and odd trails, I had to admit to myself as I spoke.

And what was worse, that meant there was nothing solid in what I was saying on which to hang a really successful series.

*

'Right then,' he said when I'd finished, 'There are things I know. Secrets I can tell you.'

'Still things that they don't want to get out?'

'Yes.'

'Like what?' I challenged. 'The scoop of the decade?'

'Please listen carefully to me. You have to understand. What I'm planning to give you won't be, how did you put it just now, "The scoop of the decade"? What I'm trying to get you to find out is probably the scoop of the century.'

'Find out? Why do you want me to find it out? If it's so big and so important to you why don't you just tell me?'

'Because, firstly, if I just told you, you simply wouldn't believe me. But secondly, and more importantly, if you did believe me and just blurted it out as a sensational story, the scoop of the century or whatever, before you've done the legwork to find the evidence, the whole thing would be dismissed as just another conspiracy theory. And then I will have wasted my time, and probably my only chance to ever get the truth out there,' he said with finality.

'So no, I'm not going to tell you. I'm going to help you look but I want you to find it yourself. To put it together, piece by piece from the files. You won't get to see the key ones of course, they'll be like the Hess ones, too highly classified and not available for years. But dedicated files on operations aren't the be all and end all. There'll be other papers that will give what you need if you know what you are looking for, meetings, cross references, inter departmental memos, committees.'

'So what am I looking for?'

'Mainly, dead ends.'

'Dead ends?' I was confused.

'Yes. This is going to be a paper trail that you are going to have to find and document. The jigsaw you are looking at is incomplete I'm afraid. It will have the vital piece missing, the picture in the centre that has been deliberately cut out. But what's left are the edges of the picture, the bits that surround the hole.'

'So you are saying that if I find all those bits, the shape of the missing picture in the middle will become obvious?'

'Yes.'

'So I'm going to be looking for a jigsaw, with no picture and the key pieces are all missing? Is that about it?'

'If you like. What you are looking for are those broken links in the trail where you run into a dead end that's a dead end because it's been deliberately closed. And when you come across enough of those, then you know that you are on to something.'

'Why? The more dead ends, the bigger the hidden secret?'

'Something like that,' he nodded. 'Committees are particularly important.'

'Committees?'

'Yes. The bigger something is, the more departments it generally cuts across and how do cross-departmental things work?'

I knew the answer to that from the files already, 'Committees?'

'Precisely.'

'And the bigger the thing, the more high powered the committee?'

'You have it.'

'But how on earth do I start to look when I don't know what I'm looking for?'

'Well you've touched close already by accident, but I will help you. I'll give you some guidance.'

'You mean you're going to shout warmer or colder as I play hide and seek with the Secret Intelligence Service files?'

'Something like that,' he smiled depreciatively, 'but probably a bit more sophisticated. So let me ask. Leaving aside all the theories about what was happening at the time and why, and whatever the truth of it was, what does the Hess thing really tell you?'

I'd seen this already. 'That we were desperate?'

He seemed pleased. 'Yes. Very good. That we were desperate, desperate for time. And you know the thing about desperate men and desperate times?'

'Desperate measures?'

'Exactly. They call for desperate measures.'

And then he gave me a history lesson. From the viewpoint of someone who'd been involved in making history happen.

'By the time we got to the autumn of 1940 and then on into '41, you have to appreciate our position.'

'Which was?'

'Essentially, we were defeated. You saw Winston's speech. We'd lost the war in Europe, but we just hadn't stopped fighting.'

'So surrender was sensible?'

'Well when you've lost, what is the sensible, obvious thing to do?'

I shrugged.

'Come to terms of course.'

'Terms?' I asked.

'Yes.'

'With the Germans?'

'Yes.'

'Surrender?

'You could call it that if you like but no, not if we could help it.'

'But was there really a deal on the table?'

'Yes,' he said calmly, 'there were indicative terms.'

'Could we have trusted them?'

'No, of course not. You could never trust anyone. But was it the sensible move to make in the short term and in those circumstances to preserve the country? Yes, it probably was.' He sat back in his chair.

'But surely Churchill would never have agreed, would he?'

'Churchill was irresponsible. Wanting to fight on, I mean,' he said.

'Irresponsible?'

'He was taking too big a risk. Hell, none of us wanted to fold to the Germans. But for the country's sake you had to put aside your own prejudices and beliefs and look objectively at the options. And if one way involves fighting on against seemingly impossible odds while another way gives a chance of independent survival for the country, then yes opting for the fighting on is an irresponsible choice.'

I sat there in silence.

'Was it really that bad?' I asked at last, 'I thought we had won the Battle of Britain over the summer...'

'Look, you have to remember that we had no experience of what it was really going to be like. When the war started we really thought we were facing Armageddon. The prevailing military doctrine at the time was Douhert's Command of the Air theory.'

I had heard about it. *The bomber will always get through* was the worry. The theory that strategic bombing of cities would rapidly lead to a country's complete collapse.

'In '39 the only example we really had was that of Guernica. Göring was a great believer in Douhert and Franco's war gave him the chance to carry out his experiment.

'We all expected the Germans to begin bombing our cities straight away from the moment war was declared. The first air raid sirens went off within half an hour of the declaration of war. All we had to go on was extrapolating casualty rates from the Zeppelin raids in the First World War and the Ministry of Health had estimated that we would suffer something like six hundred thousand dead and one point two million seriously wounded within the first six months. The military strategist Liddell Hart had said he was expecting something like two hundred and fifty thousand casualties in just the first week alone. By October 1940 it hadn't yet really happened. The Blitz had started in early September and London was burning, but we still believed it, or something like it, could be coming.'

'But we had defeated the German air force in the Battle of Britain, hadn't we?' I protested.

'Nonsense. The German *Luftwaffe* was continuing to attack Britain both night and day right through until the end of the Blitz in May 1941.'

'The threat of invasion?'

'Yes, but not just that. Even after drawing on all the empire's resources we couldn't sustain ourselves in a war with Germany.

'We were running out of money for one thing. By April 1941 our gold reserves weren't enough to cover one day's trading, so how could we afford to buy food?

'And even if we could, then there was the blockade. We were running out of food and were in real danger of simply being starved into surrender by the German navy. At the time of that speech of Winston's that you read we'd just lost thirty-two merchant ships in only three days.'

To be honest I was shocked by what he was telling me. U-boats, convoys, I'd had some vague awareness, but I'd never appreciated until now the scale of the problem in just feeding the country, or the horrific losses which had been involved in keeping us going.

'So now do you understand?' he asked.

'Something would have to be done?'

'Something would have to be done,' he nodded.

Chapter 9

Story, *n.* A narrative, commonly untrue.
The Devil's Dictionary, Ambrose Bierce

'To defeat Sealion we believed we were reliant on the Royal Navy being able to sail down the North Sea and to attack and destroy the German invasion fleet as it shuttled supplies of men and *matériel* across the channel.

'On land we had a series of stop lines; hastily constructed defensive lines of pill boxes, minefields and earthworks across the main expected invasion routes. None of these would hold the enemy for ever but each one was designed to slow him down, to buy time for the Royal Navy to reach the action.

'Then there were the stay behind squads, secret cells of local saboteurs who were only expected to last two weeks once they went underground. I heard that they were told their first job was to kill their recruiter so no one would know the cell members.

'And we think it would have worked.'

'It was played out wasn't it?' I asked, 'In the seventies?'

'Yes. We ran a full *Kriegsspiel* at the Royal Military Academy together with the Germans. The stop lines slowed them and then when the Navy came down and cut them off, the Germans became stranded with diminishing supplies.'

'But?' I added, there seemed to have been a but there.

'Well yes, but. It relied on the success of the Navy and that was the real gamble.

'If we had failed, which was a real possibility given the fleet's exposure to destruction from everything the Germans could throw at it as it came down the North Sea, then loss of the fleet could mean loss of the country, and loss of the strength that bound the empire together.

'And even if we had succeeded at an undoubtedly high cost in ships and crew, then were we likely to have failed in the long term as well. Even if we had the resources, which we were struggling with as it was, how long would it take to build new battleships to replace our losses. Particularly if the Germans concentrated on bombing the docks as they undoubtedly would. A damn site slower than it would take the Germans to build a new fleet of invasion barges and more tanks and trucks, that's for sure.'

*

'But Churchill was the Prime Minister!' I objected.

'So?'

'So that meant that you had to do what he said, he was the head of the Government, for God's sake.'

'So? Prime ministers come, prime ministers go. Governments come, governments go. Civil servants and the security services have a higher duty than just to any particular government or PM of the day. We have a duty to the nation.'

'But the government and the prime minister represent the will of the nation, don't they?'

'Yes of course. But what if they are wrong? What if the government of the day...'

'But they are the people's choice...'

'Well if I was being picky,' he said, 'I could ask who elected Churchill as war leader? The British people certainly didn't, but I won't.

'He led a national government from 1940. There was an election due but it was suspended given the war, in fact we had no general elections in Britain from '35 to '45. Other than some by-elections which tended to go against the government; as the war went on popular suffrage was effectively suspended for the duration. And what happened as soon as an election was called after the end of the war in Europe? Churchill was out and Attlee and Labour were in.

'So now tell me where was the government's popular mandate? Where was its legitimacy?

'Don't get me wrong,' he insisted. 'I admire Churchill. I really do. He was a great war leader and in the end his decision turned out to be right. But that doesn't get away from the fact that at the time, on the facts available to us in late 1940 about the situation we faced, an absolute decision to fight on regardless of the risks of defeat and destruction was in many ways madness.

'And if the prime minister is taking mad action then there is a higher duty to the nation, and yes to the people, than blind obedience.'

I was shocked, 'So do you mean you were conspiring against Churchill? Conspiring to end the war on terms with Germany?'

'No, I didn't say that.'

'But I could very well think it about others?'

'If you like.'

The room had the usual facilities, a kettle, supplies of tea bags and instant coffee granules in little sachets, and small plastic pots of UHT milk. After what he'd just said I needed a drink. He had one too.

*

'As I've said, fighting on was irresponsible. At least it was if you didn't have a plan B.'

'A plan B?'

'But actually, it was Churchill who also set up the eventual plan B, if he had but known it.'

I made the connection.

'The speech to the Press Commission?'

Sir Tom nodded, 'Yes, the speech.'

'But why to the Press Commission?' I asked. 'What on earth did that have to do with anything?'

It was as though he was ignoring the question to start with.

'A lot of people think that MI5's job is to arrest spies. That's not the case.'

'Special Branch,' I nodded.

'Yes, well, the Service doesn't actually have the powers of arrest, it uses Special Branch when it needs to but that's not what I'm getting at.

'The job is to stop spies revealing information that we want kept secret, but from early on in the war that became only half the job. Because the other half of it was to use the spies that we did catch to feed misinformation to the enemy.'

'Which is where the Double Cross system came in?'

'Precisely, the Twenty Committee who could coordinate all the things needed to make it happen successfully, from the code breakers who were reading the German decrypts of orders for despatching agents, though to MI5 and Special Branch, finding, detaining and turning them, through to SIS and their agents in enemy territory. Double Cross and the disinformation and deception it allowed us to practise was a critical and integral part of our offensive intelligence and deception war.

'Let me tell you a story. In 1939 Himmler's Intelligence Service, the SD, infiltrated our SIS operation in the Netherlands which were neutral at the time. They kidnapped two of our agents and bundled them over the border. You can look it up, it's known as the Venlo incident. The actual details of what happened aren't important for this but even after our chaps were taken, we still thought we were in contact with a real network and it's just that they had been intercepted. One of those things that happens.

'But then a fortnight later the Germans decided to blow the whistle for propaganda purposes. Ha-ha, stupid English, we took you in. All very amusing, but actually, all very stupid. We hadn't twigged. They could have played us along for as long as they wanted if they'd been careful, feeding us bits, chickenfeed, but also disinformation, misdirection. So you see...'

'Once you know...'

'We needed to buy time and have the Germans distracted. Think the unthinkable, Winston had said, and so we did.'

I looked at him in horror as he sat their quite nonchalantly.

I was seeing him in a whole new light. Not so much desk bound bureaucrat, more ice-cold killer.

*

Sir Tom wanted a refill of coffee, but proper stuff this time, not the instant muck, so we paused while I rang down for room service.

As I did so he glanced over the headlines in the paper which were all still the usual, and the latest casualty details from Basra.

It was the vehemence with which he said it that caught me by surprise almost as much as the unaccustomed raw ugliness of what he said. 'Bloody Iraqis. Churchill had the right idea.'

'Which was?'

'He wanted to bomb them with poison gas.'

'Jesus!' I exclaimed, 'Him and Saddam would have got on just fine. When the fuck was this?'

'The twenties when there was a revolt,' he said, almost absentmindedly as he devoured the front-page story, 'Churchill asked the Air Ministry if we could do it but we didn't have suitable bombs.'

Thank God for that, I thought to myself.

He shook his head at a picture of Asian Muslims at a Stop the War rally.

'I think Tebbit was onto something you know,' he said.

'What about?' I bristled, knowing what was coming.

'The cricket test.'

Which was enough, on top of everything else, to push me over the edge.

I had had just about enough of his crap by now. Growing up in Surrey, I'd run into it before. It never seemed to occur to twats like him with his military tie and cosy self-assured assumptions, that since I was white and had a home counties accent, I could be anything other than one of us, an assumed party to a casual racism about immigrants.

But the truth was, I was a second-generation immigrant. I'd had some grief about it occasionally as a kid, even some outright prejudice, but even though they didn't talk about it, I knew my parents had it worse when they'd arrived in the early '60s. Mum and Dad had come over to England at a time when there were still notices in boarding houses saying no blacks, no Irish. So fuck him, I thought.

'My parents were immigrants,' I spat, standing up.

'My Dad had cheered on anyone who was playing against England,' I said. 'He and my Mum came over here and worked for this country, he went into the Civil Service, she taught in its schools. And all he got from prats like you was crap. I've had enough of this. You can stuff your little games here, whatever they are, Sir Tom, I'm off.'

'Well it's your choice,' he said as I grabbed my bag, 'but whatever you think of me, there's more, and you know you want it.'

'What more could there possibly be to find?' I threw over my shoulder, as I headed towards the door.

'You'll see. You are almost there now. But now what you want is the hole that I talked about before. The missing piece that isn't there.'

I had my hand on the door now. It just needed a turn and I would be stepping out. Back into my life. So why was I still standing there?

'Why the hell would I listen to you?'

'Because your father would have,' he told me calmly.

Furious, I spun round to face him, 'How the hell do you know what my Dad would or wouldn't do?'

'Why don't you ask him?'

Which was a non-sequitur that stopped me in my tracks. I was still angry, but he was right in I'd come this far down the rabbit hole. I wanted to find out where it led.

'So if it's not there, how do I find it?'

'I told you, you won't find it in the British records. But then they aren't the only records, are they?'

'Such as?'

'You need to see German records.'

'Great, but I'm not in Germany, am I?' I sneered, the sarcasm heavy in my voice, 'And I don't have access to German files, do I?'

'Ah but, if you think about it, yes you do. Because there are some places where the German records are in the British ones, at least in part.'

He'd lost me now. 'Where?'

'Ultra,' he said. 'We were cracking and reading the German codes; Enigma, Lorenz and the others. The navy, army, diplomatic corps, and so on all had their different codes and machines, but we were attacking them all.'

'So I need to look at Bletchley?'

'Yes, you want an Ultra decrypt from the Bletchley files. And this,' he told me proffering a piece of paper with a reference number on it, 'is the file you need.'

I hesitated for a moment, but really, I had come this far, so reluctantly, I stepped back into the room towards where he was sitting and reaching out I tugged the note from between his fingers.

Ultra.

I was going to need to ask Libby.

*

We left the hotel separately. It was one of his rules. As I walked away towards the tube station I switched on my phone again, another of his rules, to find a number of increasingly frantic messages to call.

It was Mum, and it was a call that changed everything, for ever.

*

There was no asking Dad anything, because Dad was in hospital, and in a very bad way.

I mean, what kind of sick shit whacks an old diabetic man over the head?

It seemed to have been a burglary according to the police. Opportunistic they thought. In fact, neither Mum nor Dad had been supposed to be in at the time. Dad had an appointment at the diabetes clinic, but he'd been unwell at the last minute and had cancelled. So Mum had gone out anyway, taking the opportunity of the taxi they'd booked to head over to Brooklands and the big shops there.

I suppose whoever it was had assumed they'd both gone out.

I met Mum at his bedside and we sat listening to his raggedy breaths until late into the night, before eventually I took her home.

He never regained consciousness and died just after five the next morning.

*

I was going to need to be with Mum and give her support, that was clear. Everybody understood, the producer, Libby, everyone. I needed to take some time but I also knew I needed to keep going with what I was doing, so I left some of my research requests with Libby to find for the next time I could make it in.

And in the list I gave her was the Ultra file reference.

She didn't disappoint.

As I slid into my allotted desk a few days later for the brief stint I was allowing myself before I had to get back home to take Mum up to our bureaucratically arranged appointment to register Dad's death, I glanced through the papers she had found for me, and there it was, a German Naval Intelligence signal. It had been sent in the doubly encrypted diplomatic Floradora or Keyword code based on one-time pads, but as Sir Tom had said, we had been attacking everything and the allies had eventually broken the cypher using IBM tabulating equipment.

In truth, I barely glanced at it. What with all the rest of the things going on in my head at the time. I didn't really know why I'd come in. I wasn't really in a fit state to concentrate on anything, so all I remember registering was there were two names on it I recognised.

Top Secret

Eyes only Admiral Canaris

5th December 1940

The first was the recipient, Admiral Canaris, head of the Abwher, Germany's Military Intelligence and so Germany's chief spymaster.

> *Captured Norwegian tanker* OLE JACOB *docked Kobe yesterday under prize crew commanded by Lieutenant* KAMENZ *from surface raider* ATLANTIS *under Kapitäin-zur-See ROGGE.*

> *Lt Kamenez reports* Atlantis *engaged armed British freighter* AUTOMEDON *in the Indian Ocean 400km northwest Sumatra at 08:20 11th November. Having failed to heave to following receiving orders to do so and a warning shot the* Automedon *opened fire with three rounds from a deck mounted 100mm gun.* Atlantis *fired three broadsides in reply with her six 150mm guns devastating the bridge, the boat deck and the officers' accommodation which brought* Automedon *to a halt.*

> *Armed boarding party under Lieutenant MOHR found the Captain, Second Officer and four other officers dead and twelve*

*crew seriously wounded. Captured prisoners taken on board
Atlantis and transferred to captured tanker STORSTAD en route to
Bordeaux. Automedon sunk with scuttling charges after three-hour
search.*

*On board, Mohr's party discovered a variety of war material
including aircraft and military vehicles en route to Singapore. In the
mail room four bags were marked 'Safe Hand. By British Master
only'. When opened these were found to contain Top Secret mail for
the British High Command in the Far East including amongst other
items fleet code tables, secret notices to mariners, gunnery
instructions, Naval intelligence reports and information about
minefields and swept areas.*

*My staff are compiling a full inventory and I am arranging for
all documents to be despatched by a diplomatic courier on the next
available Trans-Siberian express.*

*In the remains of the bridge chart room the search party found
a green canvas bag, weighted and with brass eyelets for disposal at
sea, marked 'Highly Confidential – To Be Destroyed'. It would
appear that the Captain had kept it with him to be able to drop it
overboard if required but had been killed by shellfire before being
able to do so.*

*Bag contained envelope addressed to Commander in Chief Far
East [Air Chief Marshall Sir Robert Brooke-Popham]. Document
reference COS (40)592 is sent by British War Cabinet Planning
Division following meeting of British war Cabinet on 8th August
1940 and provides:*

1. *An evaluation of the strength, capabilities and readiness of
   British land, air and naval forces in Far East;*

2. *Details of defences of Singapore, main British Pacific naval
   base in Far East;*

3. *Assessment of the likelihood that Japan will enter the war in
   the Pacific on the side of the Axis; and*

4. *Assessment of the roles British dominions of Australia and New
   Zealand will be able to play in event of war with Japan in the
   Pacific.*

The document concludes in the strongest possible terms that the British are too stretched in other theatres to be able to mount a realistic and credible defence to an attack by Japan in the Pacific on the British possessions of Hong Kong, Malaya or Singapore, or to defend the Dutch East Indies whose oil production facilities would be of crucial strategic interest to Japan in the event of war.

In addition to forwarding this document to Berlin I propose providing a copy to Japanese Naval staff.

Risks:

1. *Document is a forgery, planted by the British as some form of deception. Why else would British have entrusted such a vital document to such an unlikely courier, as opposed to an armed naval vessel? Rate this as unlikely however as:*

    a. *Chances of interception by one of our commerce raiders would have been too small for British to have relied on; and*

    b. *If plan was to allow capture, no need for ship to have run risk of destruction by attempted fight and flight.*

2. *Japan will believe this is a forgery by us, designed to lure them into the war. Given the size and age of the British Empire, the Japanese will find this assessment, together with the lack of security that has allowed this to fall into our hands, as scarcely credible. However, the wealth of details, particularly concerning British order of battle and the defences of Singapore are such that the material should prove easily verifiable by the Japanese.*

I believe that revelation of the weakness of British ability to oppose any move that Japan may wish to make in the Pacific will help to:

1. *Accelerate a decision by Japan to enter the war;*

2. *Focus the Japanese thinking on America as the other Pacific power that they will face in expanding in the theatre; and*

3. *Help to form their thinking as to how best to achieve sufficient domination of the Pacific theatre before the Americans have time to react.*

I await your instructions.

Heil Hitler

Admiral Paul Wenneker,

German Naval Attaché Tokyo

And the second name was on the intercept's circulation list. It was a name I was almost expecting to see by now, one Lt T Belvoir (RN).

GC&CS – Circulation/Distribution instruction
Source – MAGIC intercept
Relevance – OPERATION CASSIUS
Forward to – Lt T Belvoir – PWE Co-Ordination Office

*

What was Operation Cassius, I remember wondering vaguely as I slipped the report back into its file? And what was the relevance of this incident? But as I said, my mind wasn't on it so I just put it away as something to come back to when I was in a state to do so, as to be honest Sir Tom and his wild goose chase wasn't top of my list of priorities at the moment.

I was more concerned with helping Mum get home back in order where the police were drawing a blank. Interrupted burglary seemed to be the hypothesis. And since despite the ransacking of the house nothing of value actually seemed to have been taken, and no significant clues left, as the days began to tick by, the generic conclusion of 'kids' and 'unsolved' had begun to hang in the air.

But all the time, try as I might to ignore it, there was something else nagging away at the back of my mind, that third name I had already come across somewhere before in some manner, shape or form, Operation Cassius.

It could wait, I thought to myself trying to put it out of my mind. It wasn't important, not with what else was going on, and anyway I told myself, it would come to me eventually.

*

Given the circumstances, there had to be a post mortem and an inquest, so the funeral was going to have to wait until the coroner released the body.

Meanwhile there were things to organise; the house to get sorted, paperwork to deal with, so I got stuck in to help Mum who had enough to face as it was.

'His death file is upstairs in the spare bedroom,' Mum told me. 'All the bank information is in there as well as things Dad always said he wanted you to see or deal with.'

Of course, there was a death file. What else would he have? How organised and practical was Dad?

I went through it sitting at the kitchen table with a cup of tea at hand, while Mum sat on the sofa in the living room next door and occupied herself by burying her head in a book. To start with it was all very prosaic, the sort of information which was always going to make it easier to help sort things out after he was gone. Details of his Civil Service pensions, which seemed a bit higher than I'd have expected for an executive officer in Customs and Excise, particularly one who'd taken early retirement on ill health, old life insurance policies, a copy of their wills, and contact details for the solicitors holding the originals.

Then there was the list of bank accounts. And I mean a list. Jesus, I thought, as I scanned down them, there were a dozen at least. Why the hell did he need to have so many accounts?

And in the last section of the file, there was the final surprise. A punched clear plastic wallet containing an envelope. And inside that, a key, to a safety deposit box at an address in Knightsbridge according to the label tied to it.

My Dad had never had a safety deposit box in his life surely, I thought, as I stared at it in silent astonishment. I opened my mouth to shout a question through to where Mum was sitting in the other room but then thought better of it.

Things Dad always said he wanted you to see or deal with hung in my head. Was this what he had meant, I wondered?

Except evidently, he had, I answered myself silently as I slipped the key into my pocket.

*

'So if there's more...?' I asked, sitting in yet another hotel room.

'There's more,' he said.

'So what do you want me to find?'

'You are close now. So close. Just a few more steps and you'll be there.'

A few more steps over the edge you mean I thought. 'This is classified stuff we are talking about here. These are Official Secrets. I could go to jail for this you know that don't you? You could go to jail. Doesn't that worry you?'

'Of course I know the risks. I was an intelligence officer for my whole career.'

'So why are you doing this. Why are we even discussing any of this?'

'You can back out any time you want. As I've said to you before I will tell you when I'm ready to.'

'This could all be a trap,' I said. 'You could still be working for the Service.'

'It's a possibility, he acknowledged with a shrug, 'At least you're starting to be paranoid enough, but really, is it one you consider likely? I didn't have to start you off down this path, did I?'

'No,' I hesitated, 'I just...'

'You'd just feel better of you knew why I was doing this?' he asked. 'I understand. And so you will, you just need the last part of the jigsaw.'

'Where do I find it?'

He looked at me for a moment, and then having made up his mind he reached down into his bag.

'Here,' he said, and proffered me a slim file he produced from its depths.

'What's this?' I asked as I took it from him.

'It's more of something you've already seen parts of before.'

'Your manuscript?' I guessed, making the connection.

'Yes,' he nodded, 'well copies of some key pages anyway.'

*

But I had one more errand in town before I went back down to see

Mum, so I hopped on a tube to Knightsbridge.

Chapter 10

Give us ten days fine weather, and England is finished.

Joseph Goebbels

As the train rattled along between stops I read the photocopied pages. It was a continuation of some of the redacted parts of Sir Tom's book I'd already seen.

*

There's very little in the British records about Operation Cassius. For obvious reasons the cover up afterwards was ruthlessly complete. For example, even in 1947 when the CinC Far East raised the question of the missing document, he was told it was believed to have been lost to U-boat action.

That was a lie, pure and simple.

*

The formal meeting had ended. Most of the delegates had left, including, I was pleased to see Hugh and Sempill, while Eden, Bruce Lockhart and a brace of their top advisors were having a wash up session, for which I had been appointed impromptu secretary and note taker.

It had quickly turned into a highly focused debate.

'…not so fast. What about Japan?'

'Well? What about it?'

'It's a member of the Axis.'

'Yes, but so far it has kept out of the war, and what's that got to do with us anyway at this stage?'

'Oh come on. The Japanese and the Americans are arch rivals for the Pacific. They've had a naval arms race going on since the Washington naval conference in the twenties. The Japanese know the Americans are thinking about blockading their oil imports and so they're looking to the Dutch East Indies as their nearest potential source of the fuel they'll need.'

'And so?'

'It's obvious isn't it? The USA and Japan will end up going to war at some point in the next few years, it seems inevitable. And when…'

'If?'

'When they do, then that will help us to make the case for the US joining in with us in our war in Europe, particularly if we were then to offer them help in the Far East. We have assets in the theatre; Singapore, Australia, the Far East fleet.'

'Fine, but the only problem is that it will be too late for us and the yanks have a strong fleet anyway, so why will they need our couple of battleships?'

'Well whatever you think of his attitude, you can't deny Hugh's basic point. It's the same issue as with Germany and Russia. Widening the war is in Britain's interests.'

'Bring in the Americans you mean?'

'Why not?'

'Because they won't come! We been through this already.'

'The Americans won't come to the rescue of Britain's Empire, true, but what if Britain and its Empire came to the aid of the US?'

'What do you mean?'

'I mean Operation Cassius.'

'We can't do that to the US!'

'Why not?'

'Because they're the ones that we want to bring in as allies for God's sake!'

'It's not as though it's unprecedented though is it? Just look at Oran. We sank the French fleet at anchor rather than run the risk of letting it fall into the enemy's hands because we had to, and they were our allies at the time…'

'And look what it did to our relationship with the French.'

'Yes, but this is war, and in war you do what is necessary.'

'True.'

'And there's no time to waste is there?'

'No.'

*

Jesus Christ, I muttered to myself, as the train burst into the light of my station and struggling to my feet against the sudden deceleration, I stuffed the papers back into my bag. Do they mean what I think they mean?

*

The proposal about Hess hung in the air as I looked across at the two men.

'You seem unsure…' Hugh started.

'Oh well that's only natural,' Bruce Lockhart chipped in towards Hugh, 'after all, as he's just said, he thinks you're a traitor. With excellent reason, I've warned him off you myself.'

Hugh laughed. 'Good man! Quite right too.'

'Young Tom here thinks you're handing secrets over to people who shouldn't have them.'

'That's practically a profession these days isn't it?' Hugh answered, which didn't exactly sound like a denial to me.

Bruce Lockhart's phone rang, he picked it up and we stayed silent as he acknowledged a summons. 'The Boss,' he explained simply, as he put down the receiver. 'We're needed at Number 10 so I'll need to leave you gents to it for the moment.'

'Are you happy to brief him?' he asked Hugh, who simply nodded. 'You're welcome to use the room.

And with that he gathered up his coat and left us to it.

*

'Secrets are currency,' Hugh began to explain as he waved me to take a seat. 'It's what you do with them that matters. Take Tizard now.

'Tizard is giving them away freely and openly to people we want to be our friends in the hope of gratitude, or at least support. And that's fine and has been sanctioned where what has been willed must be as they say.'

I nodded warily.

'And you are right, at least in part, because I'm also planning to give away secrets. But I on the other hand am going to give them to the enemy, but only after I've made them feel they have had to work to get them,

'Do you know why that is?' he asked.

'I work in intelligence, I can guess.'

'Go on…' he waited. It seemed there was nothing for it but to play his game.

'Because people only value what they've had to work to achieve. Give it to them on a plate and they don't value it, often they don't even trust it.'

'Good,' he nodded, 'so you see…'

But rather than listen, I cut across him. 'Why are you telling me this? Why trust me?

'Two reasons, one good, one bad.' He told me. 'The bad reason is I've seen your file.'

As he seemed thick with Bruce Lockhart that didn't surprise me.

'And the good?' I asked.

'You've already paid a price, more of a price than many.'

It took me a moment to realise he was taking about my brother.

'Don't you want him to have died for something?' he challenged me, before adding something which threw me completely.

'Especially given the circumstances...'

*

He explained what he meant by the circumstances.

It was a lot to take in.

He said he was sorry.

And while I dealt with that, he told me what he wanted from me.

*

'So what are you going to do with it?' I asked.

'Simple,' he said, 'I'm going to give it to Sempill.'

'Sempill, why?'

'Because Sempill really is a traitor, make no mistake about it.' Hugh said simply. 'He's both an admirer of the Nazis and a paid spy for the Japanese and he will hand it straight over to them.'

That chimed with what Bruce Lockhart had already told me about Sempill being an *aficionado* of right wing militarism, a member of anti-Semitic organisations as well as being particularly keen on cold hard cash. It also helped explained what the hell someone who'd been a known spy had been doing at the JIC meeting.

'And he'll trust it coming from you because…' but I already knew the answer to that one.

'Because he knows I'm no admirer of the Americans, so it's not been a great leap to create a view we have a shared interest when it comes to the Pacific.'

'And do you have a shared interest?' I challenged.

'Sempill is a stone-cold traitor who should be hung,' he answered bluntly.

'And yet he's being protected?'

'Yes.'

'And fed information?'

'Yes.'

'By you.'

'Yes.'

'And you openly admit it…'

'I don't openly admit it,' he said calmly, 'I'm briefing you about an ongoing operation. There's a difference.'

'Why?' I meant why did he want to recruit me, what could I provide him?

'You're a bright lad,' he smiled, 'you're in intelligence, you work it out.'

And of course, it was obvious as soon as he said it. He'd already had some from me in the report I'd delivered to him. The

Pacific was a naval theatre, so he was going to need Naval Intelligence with which to provide the chicken feed required to establish his bone fides and usefulness as a source and he wanted me to supply it. Reports, intercepts, anything which could be used to establish his credibility and to lay the ground for more important deception information later on.

'But why me?' I still wanted to know.

'You're Naval Intelligence, you're the obvious source to come to, everything of importance about naval matters comes across your desk doesn't it? So when I need, say, an amended version of something you're the best person to provide it.'

'Yes, but why use me? I'm not the only one. Why not Fleming for instance?' I suggested.

'He's too keen on the yanks, and he's a bit of a fantasist,' he said dismissively. 'I'm not sure I'd trust him with something like this.'

'Besides which, there's something else I might need your help with,' he added.

'What's that?' I asked.

'The Brooke-Popham memo, do you know what's in it?' he asked me.

'I've heard rumours, but nothing definite.'

'It hasn't been despatched yet,' he told me, which was strange as it dated back to early August and we were now approaching the end of October. 'I'm holding onto it at the moment.'

'Why?' I wanted to know.

'So I can find a way of making sure the Germans get it,' he told me flatly. His problem was he wasn't sure how to manage it in a way that would work.

He didn't want to use Sempill as he wanted to spread the channels he was using. Having the enemy receive information from a number of sources always looked more convincing than having just one. I suggested the Double Cross network but he'd already rejected it as too busy, and its operatives being too low level. This was something that would be way above any of their agent's reach.

But even so, I reminded myself pulling back, we were sitting here in the middle of Whitehall discussing leaking a top-secret Cabinet Office report to the enemy.

'Are you mad?'

'No, and the PM will confirm if you want him to.'

He handed me a phone. 'Go on. Call him. Say you're calling from Bruce Lockhart's office, they'll put you through.'

I knew he was right, they would, but even so. Winston was always a fan of bizarre operations. Gallipoli. Zeebrugge, and I'd heard him deliver our mandate for myself.

Thinking the unthinkable was only the start of it. Now as I put the receiver down without dialling, we had to do it.

*

It had been Charlie's first raid. And his last.

Of all the Hampdens ever built, almost half were lost in action, taking with them over eighteen hundred aircrew killed or missing.

One of which was Charlie. That much I already knew.

What I didn't understand until then was what Hugh had meant by *given the circumstances.*

Not until Hugh had explained them to me.

But I didn't just take them from him. Back in the office I shared with the RAF officer I asked him to dig out the post action report, to find, when it came the following day that Hugh was right all along.

According to the RAF's own later estimates, by 1941 once the bombing campaign had started in earnest against the Ruhr valley and Germany's industrial heartland, only one in ten of our bombers was getting within five miles of their targets, and about fifty percent of all bombs ended up falling on open country.

The raid my brother had been on was no exception.

The target had been naval facilities on the island of Sylt just off Germany's North Sea coast, but his part of the raid went nowhere close.

According to the follow-up reconnaissance photo flights, my brother had actually died bombing a field of cabbages.

As I handed the file back to my colleague with muttered thanks, all I could think of were Hugh's angry words from The Meeting about the American's attitude still ringing in his ears. *Goodwill is all very well, but I'd rather have a working bombsight. If you can't use it to drop a bomb down a Ruhr factory chimney, what use is it to us?*

I sat at my desk, leafing blankly through the latest crop of Ultra Kriegsmarine intercepts. I wasn't really reading them, there was too much going on in my head. To this day I still don't know why that particular signal stuck out from all the rest. It was a routine report, an update on his position and intentions from the commander of an obscure commerce raider.

What was it Winston always used to say? *Carpe diem? Carpe diem* indeed.

Seized with a sudden sense of determination I picked it up and went in search of Hugh.

'I'm in,' I said, marching into his room after the briefest of knocks. 'And I have an idea…'

*

The address turned out to be a discreet looking door just across the way from Harrods.

Deep in the bowels of the earth half an hour or so later I sat in the cubicle, the contents of the box on the table in front of me, and everything I thought I knew about my world was crashing down around my ears.

Dad had been a Customs Officer, we'd all known that as we'd grown up. He'd wanted to go to university, and then join the RAF, but given the family's desperate need for money, he'd had no choice but to abandon those ambitions in favour of bringing in another steady income. So he'd followed his father into the Royal Ulster Constabulary straight from school, one of a very few young Catholics to do so, and lasted a few years until he'd met Mum, from a Protestant farming family, and they'd come to England at the turn of the sixties. He'd taken the Civil Service exam and come sixth nationally and ended up as a Customs Officer, first at London docks and then at Heathrow airport until his early retirement on health grounds, which was why we'd been brought up in London and then Surrey.

Or so we'd always been told.

But not according to what I had here.

These papers told a very different story about what use the British government could make of a bright young man with a police background, who wasn't from a public school and Oxbridge background at the opening of the sixties. A young man who could slip into working at London docks as they began to close down, at a time when its radical shop stewards were the centre of communist trade unionist activity in the country. Someone who could turn up to listen to the rabble-rousing speeches of the likes of dockers' leader Jack Dash, the Arthur Scargill of his times.

And then as the sixties drew to a close of course, such a man who was also catholic, with a knowledge of Ireland would become valuable for a whole new set of reasons. Giving in the end very different reasons for an early retirement, for a very good pension income which I'd never really questioned, and for an ongoing and incisive interest in politics, the behind the scenes machinations and conspiracy theories.

Dad, someone who never used his own name had, according to this box, had a very different life from what we'd ever been told, as a serving officer in MI5.

Which made me wonder. Who had really broken in? And what had they really been after?

And who had Dad known?

*

The very next day, given our discussions, I had another report I had produced which I thought was worthwhile taking across to Hugh's office.

Top Secret

Memorandum

Sunday 27th October 1940

As per the attached intercept, the Japanese have asked the Judo network to actively seek information about any research we may have conducted into the use of aerial launched torpedoes, particularly for use in shallow waters.

It is our assessment that the Japanese are interested in learning about the technical modifications made, although Japanese service aircraft are all of far more modern design than our Swordfish and consequently fly much faster.

As already discussed, the modifications made and currently being further developed are in reality quite simple.

The technique we currently employ is to keep the torpedo nose up prior to entering the water through use of a wire trailing from the aircraft.

We believe the desired effect can also be achieved for faster flying aircraft by the application of:

1. *Detachable wooden fins attached to the tail of the torpedo to keep the nose level in the air as it is dropped. The flatter flight trajectory means the torpedo enters the water at a much shallower angle than normal and therefore dives less deeply, while the fins and a wooden nosecone designed to cushion the impact break off on impact with the sea.*
2. *Anti-roll flippers to keep the torpedo upright once it's in the water.*

Both of these approaches are quite straightforward and reasonably obvious solutions to the problem which can be discovered with little difficulty once the requirements are studied. We therefore believe that the Japanese will quickly work these modifications out for themselves, with or without our help.

I therefore believe that in giving the Japanese what they are looking for we will be doing ourselves no meaningful harm, but we will on the other hand be firmly establishing the Judo system's bona fides in their eyes.

I therefore propose that this torpedo information is appropriate chickenfeed to deliver in order to build the Judo network's credibility and request your authorisation to arrange the release of suitable material.

*

'This has been willed where what has been willed must be,' Hugh joked, as he signed his approval over my signature and recommendation, before adding his instructions to Expedite Forthwith. 'And as you're here, I've thought about your suggestion yesterday. Do you really think he'd do it?'

'Yes, Sir, I do,' I said, picking up the file to return to its sender.

'Well in that case I think we need to ask him straight away. We've no time to lose if we're going to make your plan work, so I suggest we arrange to see him today,' Hugh announced. 'Is that alright with you?'

'Yes,' I told him.

'No second thoughts?'

'No.'

'Very well then, and Tom,' he added.

'Yes, Sir?'

'Welcome to the pit of evil counsellors.'

*

There was certainly one person I was going to need to ask, I decided, as I carefully replaced most of the papers in the box and returned it to the commissionaire.

'Is there a photocopier I could use before we put this away again?' I asked. He nodded and directed me to a door just off the hall labelled Business Services.

And there was one person I certainly wasn't going to tell, not at this stage yet at least, I decided as I stepped back out onto the street a few minutes later, thinking about Mum waiting for me back at home.

This was on a need to know basis.

*

We left Whitehall at lunchtime heading for the coast, and having had our yes later that afternoon, we swung straight into action. Signals were sent and with Hugh's authority a military flight was swiftly arranged which would hop its way down to South Africa, while coded signals went out to meet the ship.

As we swayed back up towards London in the blacked-out train we had a reserved compartment.

'What do we do now?' I asked, as we crawled the final miles into Waterloo.

'We wait.' he said calmly. 'It's all we can do.'

'Hopefully we'll have just managed to give then all the political and strategic clearance they could ever hope for. We'll set them the example and we'll even have shared how we did it. Now it's up to them.'

'How long?'

'I'd give it six months, a year at the outside.'

*

The Germans delivered the Brooke-Popham memo captured from the *Automedon* to the Japanese on the 5th December 1940.

Chapter 11

It's much easier to get water into a ship from the bottom than
the top.

Quote attributed to an American Admiral
on the difference between torpedoes and bombs

'You knew my father, didn't you?' I demanded, as I sat down in Sir
Tom's study again. I hadn't rung or made an appointment. I'd just driven
up to his house and rung the bell until he'd answered the door.

We were sitting exactly where we'd started our conversation three
months before. Very little had changed in his room, other than the
arrival of a white plastic box of a photocopier which now squatted in the
far corner of the room.

At first he hadn't wanted to let me in, but as I held up Dad's Service
record where he could read it, eventually he saw I wasn't going to take
no for an answer and opened the door.

'Knew him?' Sir Tom smiled, as he showed me through and gestured me
to take the same seat as I'd had before. 'I recruited him. Did you work
that out, or did he tell you?'

I shrugged.

'And you knew who I was didn't you? Right from the outset?'

'Well it doesn't matter now I suppose,' he said sounding amused, 'but of
course. He wrote to me when he heard about your series. Said it might
be the opportunity I'd been waiting for. Why else do you think I decided
to talk to you of all people?'

'And give me your run around?' I accused, 'Hints here and there, secret
squirrel meetings.'

'Ah, but why do you think I've given you the run around, as you put it?'
he asked.

He didn't have to tell me. I'd worked out the answer to that myself
already. 'It's like you said about the Japanese. If I find the pieces myself
from here and there and fit them together I'll believe it more than if it
was just laid out in front of me. I've made the emotional investment on

the effort of discovery that predisposes me to believe it.'

'That's right...' he nodded approvingly.

'And so we'd be safe to talk,' I added.

'Yes.'

'So are we safe now? I asked.

'Here?'

I nodded.

'Oh yes, quite safe,' he said calmly.

'How do you know?'

'I had it swept. I still have friends in the Service.' He had to have I realised. Otherwise how had he managed to arrange for me to see the papers I had? Someone on the inside had to have been working with him to make those available. 'People I trust. Friends who think like I do. Who agree that it's time we were free, independent, able to go our own way...'

'Who?'

'The Services aren't a homogenous mass you know. There are differences...'

'Factions?'

'If you like. You have the Peter Wright, *Spycatcher* mob. The right wingers bugging and burgling their way across London who were hell-bent on taking down Harold Wilson because they believed he was a Russian agent.'

'And there are others?'

He nodded. 'Yes, others who aren't happy with the way intelligence is being used today, prostituted and abused for political ends. The Service's reputation has been dragged through the mud. So you can see why a lot of people would be very unhappy about that.'

'And it was clean?' I asked, 'Your office?'

'There was nothing, but then I wasn't expecting anything.'

'Why not?'

'Because I'm not regarded as a security risk of course.' He said it as though it was too obvious to be true and of course, in many ways it was. 'I'm one of us. I've been seen to be keeping them informed. I've years of loyal service behind me. I'm regarded as a solid chap, a good soldier.'

He regarded me as I sat there quietly waiting for him.

'So what did you find?' he asked at last.

'You know what I found don't you?'

'I think so.'

'Operation Cassius. Why don't you tell me about Operation Cassius?'

*

Had they but known it, they had been picked up on radar as they made their approach.

But their luck held. The detection system was new and unreliable so its operation at this stage was still regarded as being largely just a training and debugging exercise. The staff only worked limited hours and reported their findings to a control centre which was equally incidental to how the defences were being operated.

As it happened, that morning the radar operators' breakfast truck ran late so they didn't shut down on time at 07:00 sharp as they would normally have done, and picked up the first of the signals at 07:02.

However, when they called through their report, since the control centre was operating on a well organised site, all the staff they needed to speak to had already left for their breakfast which was served at 07:00 on the dot. No one was on duty to take the call apart from a single lieutenant trainee on his second day, who'd never had a briefing on what to do with any information which came in, and no contact with any of the airfields which could be scrambled in any case.

Not that the planes on the airfields were in a position to be scrambled anyway. Instead fear of sabotage had led them to be drawn up in neat rows in the middle of the runways so as to be easier to guard.

As the incoming armada of first wave aircraft flew on under strict radio silence, the blazing early morning sun was already rising in a beautifully clear sky above a low layer of concealing cloud. At the head of the flight of level bombers their commander listened intently to the reconnaissance reports of two planes ahead and monitored the radio traffic coming from the target so as to make his decision about the critical signal he would soon need to make. One rocket for the surprise plan, and two rockets for surprise lost.

Now as they powered on down the coast towards their attack deployment start lines, he had to choose, and raising his signal pistol aloft through his opened cockpit he fired. A single trail of black smoke, and at once while circling their rendezvous point the planes began to diverge. The fifty-one dive bombers began to climb upwards, heading for 12,000 feet, the fifty level bombers circled downwards to 3,500 feet, while the forty torpedo planes with their weapons newly modified to work in the shallow waters of the harbour, headed further down towards just above wave height.

They would have the honour of actually leading the attack so as to have the best view before smoke began to obscure the scene.

The unsuspecting objective was only a few minutes flying time away now, and once each group of aircraft had reached their operating altitudes, they turned as a body for their run in to their individual targets which were becoming easily visible ahead in the rapidly breaking cloud of what had all the makings of a beautiful clear morning.

*

'You've read the papers I gave you?' he asked.

'Yes.'

'Then I don't need to tell you about Operation Cassius. You have it all there.'

'I have some of the pieces,' I told him carefully. 'But that's the thing about jigsaws isn't it? I just need to make sure I'm fitting them into the right picture, or not.

'And even if they're all pointing the same way, I still know I have some gaps which is why I want to hear it from you. In full, just so as there's no confusion.'

*

The annual Army-Navy game of American football is a fixture

of US sports, but the 29th November 1941 match played at Franklin Memorial Stadium in Philadelphia, Pennsylvania is today famous, or rather infamous, more for one page of the 212-page programme, than the result.

Given the international circumstances at the time it's perhaps not surprising that alongside the profiles of each of the squads, the publication featured numerous photographs and articles on each of the forces and their military preparedness.

In particular page 180 carried a classic battleship photograph accompanied by the caption, *A bow on view of the* USS Arizona *as she plows into a huge swell. It is significant that despite the claims of air enthusiasts no battleship has yet been sunk by bombs.*

The only problem was, ignoring even the British example at Taranto the previous year using torpedoes, the America military should have known this statement simply was not true.

The reason? They had sunk battleships themselves in bombing tests twenty years earlier.

Having already sent the ex-German destroyer *G-102* and the ex-German light cruiser *Frankfurt* to the bottom, in a somewhat fractiously organised test involving bombing by Navy, Marine Corp and Army aircraft over two days in July 1921, the ex-German World War I battleship, *Ostfriesland* was sunk 50 miles off Chesapeake Bay. Billy Mitchell's First Provisional Air Brigade then went on to repeat the exercise by sinking the pre-dreadnought *Alabama* in September 1921, and the obsolete battleships *Virginia* and *New Jersey* in September 1923.

And of course, just a week after the game itself, on the morning of 7th December 1941, Japanese bombers came roaring in out of a clear Hawaiian blue Sunday morning sky, taking the sitting US Pacific fleet completely by surprise. To cut through the battleship's decks, fins had been welded onto 16-inch artillery shells turning them into highly effective armour piercing bombs as they whistled down from 9,800 feet. The *Arizona* was bombed from amidships to the stern by a first flight of bombers, then on the bow by a second.

Just after 08:00 she suffered three direct hits which caused damage and started fires. Then at about 08:06 she was hit a fourth time, this time the bomb penetrated the deck in the vicinity of the second turret. For five or six seconds nothing happened, and then the forward magazines detonated in a cataclysmic explosion.

Effectively ripped in two, the battleship sank immediately with 1,177 fatalities.

The wreck remains a war grave and a memorial at Pearl Harbour to this day.

*

'What gaps do you think you have?' he asked.

'Well there's reference in the papers you gave me to a missing document which seems to have been important. Certainly important enough for its loss to have been covered up both during, and then after the war. Long after.'

'You know the one I mean,' I told him, as I watched his face. 'It's the smoking gun isn't it?'

He nodded in acknowledgement.

'So what was it?' I asked. 'What was so important about this particular bit of paper?'

'It's called the Brooke-Popham memo,' he replied, 'and it was the final thing the Japanese navy needed. It was the document that told the Japanese they were clear to attack, that there was nothing we could do in the theatre to support the Americans.'

*

What Kapitän zur See Bernhard Rogge and Lieutenant Ulrich Mohr poured over in Rogge's quarters that afternoon was something that shocked both of them to the core in terms of its potential importance. They held in their hands a twenty-eight-page briefing document prepared by the War Cabinet's Planning Division. It gave the latest assessment of the respective Japanese and British military strength in the Far East, right down to notes on the strength and available equipment of individual naval and RAF units, as well as Singapore's defences, and Australia and New Zealand's potential roles in any conflict.

Drawn up as a result of a War Cabinet discussion on the 8th August 1940 the memo discussed the possibility of Japan entering the war, and summarised the lack of British men and material in the theatre to deal with such a threat. As a result, the Cabinet had concluded that the British Empire was simply and unequivocally in no position to mount a credible defence if the Japanese were to

164

attack British possessions in the region or the Dutch East Indies, modern day Indonesia.

*

I had been right. In many ways it was the final piece in the jigsaw, the one that made sense of all the others.

'But you couldn't have had anything to do with them getting hold of it, surely?' I protested, 'I mean it was seized by chance by that German raider. There was no way...'

Although even as I said it I realised that of course there was a way of knowing where and when a German raider was stalking the sea lanes. The Ultra intercepts that crossed the desks of naval intelligence officers every day, officers like one Lieutenant Tom Belvoir.

'But even if...' I started, but Sir Tom wasn't listening.

He had closed his eyes and I could see he was somewhere else.

'So who was he?' I asked at last. 'He must have been a brave man to trail his coat like that.'

'He was the bravest man I ever met, and he knew the risks,' Sir Tom said.

'Even so, there's a difference between knowing the risks and going to almost certain death. So who was he?'

And the answer shocked me.

'He was my father.'

*

At my blackest moments I just have to close my eyes and I imagine the final scenes on board the *Automedon* that day. The *Atlantis'* guns shelling the ship, and up on the bridge, my father being killed.

*

As Hugh had said the problem was simple. The Japanese needed to see the memo so we needed a mechanism to get it to them. But it had to be a different source to the other material they'd been receiving. They had to be made to feel they were getting multiple independent and verifiable leads, and the Germans had to be made to feel they had worked to win it. They couldn't just be handed it on a plate.

'We have a problem with the Ultra intercepts we're receiving,' I told Hugh. 'The very quality and quantity of them gives us a dilemma. It's all very well knowing where their raiders and U-boat packs are but it's not information we can actually use most of the time. If we simply move all our convoys out of harm's way then it would do us some good in the short term but in the long run it would give away that we could read their messages.

He sat back in his chair, waiting for me to tell him something he didn't know.

'But what if we could use it to put something in their way? Something we wanted them to find?'

'You mean the memo?' he asked.

'Precisely. Put it on a ship and arrange for it to be taken.'

'They'd have to put up a fight.'

'Yes, enough to make it look realistic.'

'Against a German commerce raider?' he snorted, 'It would be a suicide mission.'

'Yes.'

'Where would you get the men for it?' he demanded, 'You can't ask men to go to almost certain death like that?'

'Perhaps you can, Sir.'

*

It was true, you couldn't really ask men to go and die for you, unless of course, they already knew they were going to die.

Then you could ask them to make it mean something. Which was why late that Sunday afternoon I found myself leading Hugh into the ward at the Seamen's Hospital down in Portsmouth to sit down by the side of my father's bed.

I made the introductions and my father sat up against the pillows which were propping him up as he sized up Hugh, before switching his gaze to me as he asked what we wanted.

'We're here to offer you a cruise,' I told him, 'somewhere warm, if you want it.'

'Oh yes?' he said with a sharply raised eyebrow. 'And the catch is?'

'The thing is,' I told him, 'it's likely to be a one-way trip.'

He didn't flinch a jot.

'I see,' he said settling back into his bed, 'Well as it happens that's something I'm on here, son. So what do you have in mind?'

In quiet voices we told him the plan.

'I'd need a crew,' he said, 'officers at least, and they'd need to know what they were signing up for.'

He was right. It wasn't just him who would be at risk. It was all very well finding him but just one man wasn't enough. We needed half a dozen or so, but where were we going to get them?

'Well son, I guess you just have to look around you,' he said and then raising his voice he called out to the rest of the ward.

'Listen up,' he barked, 'man here's got a proposition for you all.'

Half a dozen faces turned to look in our direction from the beds down the ward as Hugh and I stood up to face them.

'We're looking for volunteers,' I announced. 'For a mission down in the Indian Ocean. It's a dangerous job as you'll be tugging a tiger's tail and we don't expect many, if any of you, to come back, which is why we're only asking men who are in your condition.'

It wasn't an attractive pitch, but then in my defence, it wasn't one I had intended to make.

'You would be doing your country an immeasurable service, a live or die one that no one will ever be able to know about,' Hugh added calmly, as he appeared at my elbow and we asked for a show of hands.

And bless them all, every single man in the ward raised his hand.

'We're all in the same boat here more or less,' the chap in the bed next to my father joked, 'We might as well be in the same boat somewhere warm I reckon.

*

'I'm sorry,' I told him when he'd finished speaking.

'Yes, well, I'm sorry too,' he replied, 'we've both lost people in connection with this, and we never meant that to happen.'

But I wasn't really listening.

*

'So you need to tell me everything,' I said, as I picked up my bag from beside where I was sitting and pulled out my iPad.

'Everything?'

'Yes, the how, the why…' I hesitated as the implications sank in, 'My God, the why?'

'The why? I would have thought that was obvious.'

I checked the charge, there was plenty to be able to record for a while and I looked around the room for a suitable spot.

'So tell me. And then you're going to have to tell me something else.'

'What's that?' he wanted to know as he watched me getting organised without any objection.

'The why are we talking now. The why you are doing this, now after all these years. The why I'm involved in this, and then the what the hell you're expecting me to do about this afterwards.'

'Oh that,' he said dismissively, 'Well that's quite simple.'

'Is it?' I asked as I stood up.

'Oh yes. Broadcast dear boy. Broadcast and tell the public. Educate and inform, it's what the BBC's there for isn't it?'

'My God. You are actually serious, aren't you?'

'Absolutely.'

Checking the view covered where he was sitting I arranged my iPad on the desk beside us and set it running.

'And now you want to go on the record,' I said, as I sat down again. 'Is that it?'

'Certainly,' he said calmly, nodding at the silent lens facing him at more or less eye level from the desk.

'So Sir Tom Belvoir,' I started, 'for the record. Please tell me what Operation Cassius was, and how it worked?'

'Operation Cassius was a plan developed and implemented in late 1940 by certain members of the Secret Intelligence community of His Majesty's Government.'

'And this document that I have a copy of here,' I said, brandishing a copy I'd made of the photocopy I'd smuggled out of the Registry, 'is a minute of the committee that drew up this plan. Is that correct?'

'Yes, it is.'

'And who was on that committee?'

'The people named in that document.'

'Does that include you?'

There was a moment's silence before in a strong certain voice he said.

'Yes, it does.'

'And the objective of that plan?' I asked.

This was the big one. But he didn't even hesitate.

'It was to secretly precipitate and to bring about, an attack by the Japanese Empire upon the United States, so as to bring the United States of America into the war on our side.'

'Were you specifically encouraging the Japanese to attack the American fleet at Pearl Harbour?'

'Yes.'

'Why?'

As he put it, the reasons were very simple.

'If we continued to stand alone, the chances were, no, the certainty was, we would lose. Either by being invaded, or by Germany starving us out. If Russia and Germany were to go to war, this would buy us time, distracting Germany from mounting an invasion, but we did not believe it would save us of itself.

'But if America also entered the war with her manpower and industrial might, then that would change everything. Our chances of survival and of winning the war would improve dramatically.

'So that's what we needed to see happen. The logic was inescapable. The only questions were, how were we going to go about it?'

I stayed silent, letting him speak. This was his moment, his opportunity to explain in his own words. I wanted him to have it.

'We needed to bring the United States into the war. And while we knew the Japanese were going to continue to expand aggressively in the Far East, and were likely to eventually end up in a conflict with the Americans, in the short term there was no actual need or reason for them to attack the US. They could start by taking what they wanted from European countries' possessions in the region to build up their strength before taking on the Americans, secure in the knowledge we were otherwise engaged.

'The main thrust of the Japanese Army's plans for attack were always to be southwards, down through British Malaya for tin and rubber, and towards Batavia, the Dutch East Indies for oil, not east towards the US.

'If you think about it, what lies eastwards from Japan across the Pacific before you get to Hawaii?'

'Not much,' I offered.

'Precisely, a vast expanse of empty ocean and a few rocks of little productive value. No, we couldn't rely on Japan taking on the United States when she attacked us, we knew that. So, if we wanted America to enter the war in the near future we had to do something to make sure they were dragged in.'

'And you decided on Pearl Harbour?'

'Yes.'

'Why?'

'It was always going to be the Japanese navy who would fight the Americans in the end, and every naval country's main concern in those days was the strength of their enemy's battleship fleet. It's why the Americans wanted us to send our fleet to Canada in early 1940, and why we seized or sank as much of the French fleet as we could after the French surrender. We both wanted to avoid capital ships falling into enemy hands.

'So we worked to give the Japanese navy a plan to help speed up what was always going to happen by showing them how to neutralize the main threat they felt they faced, the American battleships in the Pacific.'

'And how did you do that?' I asked. I wanted him to spell out exactly what they had done.

'In practice we'd already shown them what could be done. We'd attacked and sunk French battleships at anchor at Oran in July 1940. We did the same with the Italians at Taranto. How much more of an example did we need to give the Japanese navy what they needed to do to destroy an enemy's fleet?'

'They were ordinary operations undertaken on their own merits, weren't they? But you went further than that didn't you?'

'Yes, each of those actions was taken for its own strategic reasons. But we then used them as a starting point. If sinking the enemy's battleships were what Japan's navy thought they would need to do to gain a decisive advantage in a Pacific war, then we decided to show them how they could do it to encourage them to take action.'

'So there were leaks about torpedo technology, and how they could be used in shallow water attacks by aircraft?'

'Yes, that was the how, and we also had to show them they had the opportunity.'

'Which is where the Brooke-Popham memo fitted in?' I prompted.

'Quite. That report spelt out that there was little if anything we could do to oppose Japanese aggression in the Far East. Effectively it told the Japanese they had a free hand, they didn't have to worry about us and so the only real potential enemy they faced were the Americans.'

'You realized it painted a target on the USA, and then made sure it fell into Japanese hands?'

'That's exactly what we did. We wanted to provoke a Japanese attack on America which would bring them into the war on our side against the Axis powers and get their support in defending our empire in the Far East.

'And so we gave the Japanese navy what they needed,' he said, counting off his points on his hand.

'One, we confirmed to them their need to decide when to go. Their agents had sight of the McCollum memo, briefing on the American plans to tighten the noose and weaken Japan for when the US did eventually go to war. It told the Japanese navy they could wait and be weakened, or they could choose their moment to strike first.

'Two, the examples of what to do. Oran and Taranto; how it was possible to take out an enemy fleet at harbour.

'Three, the how to do it. The basic details of how to adapt aerial torpedoes for attacks in shallow harbour waters.

'Fourth, and finally, the comfort that if they went ahead, we weren't a threat they would need to worry about, the Cabinet Office's report to our CinC in the Far East.'

He sat back in his chair. 'After that, it was up to them.'

'Well it worked,' I observed.

'No, it didn't,' he hissed sharply. 'Don't you understand? As a plan it failed utterly. All of it.'

Chapter 12

Now we have an ally that has not lost a war in 3,000 years!
Adolph Hitler

'I can't tell you what the panic was like afterwards across Whitehall amongst those of us involved,' he said.

After Pearl Harbour? After FDR's famous Act of Infamy speech? After what they'd done? I thought. I was struggling to put into words what I felt. 'I think I can imagine the reaction. Something like *Oh My God, this must never get out, never, you understand?*'

'Well yes,' he conceded, 'but more than that.'

'What?

'Well because in the immediate aftermath, there was only one clear fact we were concerned with, which was that it simply hadn't worked. The real panic was that the US didn't immediately declare war.'

'On Germany?'

'Exactly,' he nodded. 'And not even on Japan to start with. In fact since they'd launched a simultaneous invasion of Malaya we declared war on them almost nine hours before the Americans did.

'We thought that by siding so publicly with the US we might help tip the balance towards them reciprocating by coming into our war on Germany and the Axis powers as a block. After all, that had been the while point of Operation Cassius from its inception.

'But even that wasn't enough, and the Americans still only declared war against Japan when they finally came in on 8 December, the day after the attack. Despite everything we'd done, we were still facing a Nazi Germany which had already rolled the Russians back to the gates of Moscow, without the United States on our side.'

'And that's why you say the operation was a failure?' I checked.

'That, and other reasons,' he replied.

*

'But you got what you wanted,' I insisted, 'The Americans came into the war on our side.'

He shook his head. 'What was it that Winston always used to say? *You can rely on America to do the right thing, but only after all other options have been eliminated.'*

'But they did come into the war,' I repeated, 'they did fight on our side.'

'Oh yes, yes they did,' he said bitterly. 'And we have one man to thank for that.'

'Who?' I was confused. 'You mean Roosevelt?'

'No not Roosevelt!' he sounded exasperated. 'Honestly, what sort of history do they teach you kids today?'

He nodded at my phone, 'You've internet access on that thing, haven't you? Look it up.'

As I unlocked my phone and typed in my search he carried on talking.

'The Japanese attack had destroyed much of the US Pacific fleet except for the carriers which were out on exercise. We'd started a war all right. But a separate war, one we would be drawn into to defend our Far East possessions, diverting resources and making ourselves weaker at home while still facing the German menace across the channel. It was looking like the worst of all possible worlds.'

'But even so, they did come into the war... Ah here we are,' I said, as I found the relevant entries on Wikipedia and started to read.

'Yes, they did.'

'Oh my God,' I said, under my breath as I read and suddenly realised what he was saying.

'So what does it tell you there?' he demanded.

'On 11 December Germany declared war on the USA,' I read out to him.

'Precisely!' he emphasised. 'Adolf Hitler is the man we have to thank for helping us out of the trap we had dug for ourselves. Thank God for the whims of Adolf Hitler and his decision to declare war on the US.'

'Not the other way round...' I nodded, still reading.

'No, not the other way round,' he confirmed. 'That's what I'm trying to tell you. We failed. We started a war in which millions would die, and we had failed in the single objective, the one reason that we had staked all on provoking the clash.

'The Americans decided to fight all right. It's just they didn't decide to fight who we wanted them to.

'If it wasn't for Hitler and his seizing the initiative, the Americans could have just left us and the Germans alone to get on with it. Indeed, that's exactly what they did do for four days after Pearl Harbour until Hitler seemingly on a whim made all the difference.'

*

'But even so, it worked in the end though didn't it?' I asked. 'The Americans did come in on our side, and we won the war in the end…'

'Did we?' he asked. 'I suppose it depends on who you mean by we.

'Russia defeated Germany. Don't let anyone fool you. It was the Russians, at a cost. About thirty million deaths by some counts.

'And the Pacific was a disaster to start with. Only three days after Pearl Harbour, Japanese aircraft sank the battleship *HMS Prince of Wales* and the battlecruiser *HMS Repulse* with the loss of 840 hands, effectively destroying our Eastern fleet in one blow. We lost Singapore, we lost Malaysia, the Dutch lost what's now Indonesia, the Americans lost the Philippines, the French lost Indochina. We damn nearly lost Burma, and if we had, India would have been next. The Japanese got to New Guinea and were bombing Australia.'

'But yes,' he conceded, 'in the end the Allies did defeat the Germans, and the Japanese. And what was the final result?'

'The end of the war?' I said, confused by what he meant.

'No, for us, for Britain? Don't you ever ask yourself that?'

'Like I said, the end of the war.'

'But what about the country's interests?' he insisted.

'Russia dominated half of Europe and we were bankrupted,' he confirmed. 'Churchill had to go down on his knees and plead to FDR for food. We become a vassal state to the US and lost the empire anyway.

'We got everything we wanted, and yet we still lost everything we wanted to preserve, our independent place in the world and our empire.

'The cornerstone of British foreign policy for centuries had been maintaining the balance of power in Europe. But the world was more than Europe by the end of the war, it had become a global world, with global powers with their own interests and modern empires.

'We sowed the seeds of our own destruction. We weakened ourselves and helped wake sleeping giants.'

Is this why you are telling me this? I wondered, as he spoke. Because we lost the empire? There had to be more to it than this.

*

And all I still wanted to know was why.

In all his explanations he'd still not answered the one real question I had. And it wasn't about the war. It was about the here and now. This was a story he had known for over sixty years now, so what had changed to make him talk now?

'I need to know whether you are playing me,' I challenged him. 'I need to know why you are telling me this and what's in it for you?'

'Haven't you been listening to what I've said, don't you realise what I'm telling you is true? What does it matter why I'm talking now? I'm an old man, have you thought of that?'

'It matters, Sir Tom,' I said flatly, 'as you know full well.

'Because until I know what's in it for you, I don't know what's in it for me, do I? If I don't know your agenda, how do I know whether I'm being set up for the biggest pratfall in journalistic history, or whether you really want me to cause the biggest diplomatic incident of this century?'

We stared across at each other as I spoke.

'You've had over sixty years within which to tell this story if you felt it was so important, but you've stayed silent all that time. So I need to know why now? What's made such a difference that you are going to break the trust and the habits of a lifetime. To go against everything you've been trained in and believed in. To betray the confidences and secrets you've kept all these years?'

'There has to have been something. You don't just wake up one morning, or read a letter from my Dad and decide to go against

176

everything you have ever stood for, do you?

'So there has to be something, something that matters to you enough to make this happen. And for me to believe, I need to know what that something is.'

He sat quietly in his chair after I had finished. I let the silence grow.

'Very well,' he said at last in a weary voice. 'You are right of course. Service. Duty to the state, call it what you will. It is in my blood. Literally you know. Literally.'

I knew. The sacrifices his family had made, for king, for country, for the now long-gone empire.

Reaching onto the desk he opened an envelope and handed me a photo. It was a small group shot, Sir Tom, as ever in jacket and military tie, a young man in a smart officer's uniform, a smiling young woman that I recognised and two young children.

I look up at him again, suddenly seeing him again for the frail elderly man he was and dreading what was coming next.

'My grandson and his family,' he told me.

'I met his wife.'

'Yes you did,' he nodded, 'She was just leaving when you first arrived.'

It had been a happy occasion. Summer sunshine by the look of it. They were all smiling for the camera and you could see the pride in each of their faces.

'His passing out parade?' I guessed.

'Yes.'

I passed the photograph back to him and he stared at it blindly for a few moments, as if he had never seen it before.

'Why are you showing me this?' I asked gently.

But he didn't answer me directly.

'For over half a century we as a country have been blindly following the US lead. And have you ever asked yourself for what? Why? For the basic reason, we can't afford not to. Why do we carry their nukes for them on our submarines? Why were we their forward nuclear base against

Russia during the height of the cold war and one of Russia's main nuclear targets?

'It took us into the cold war and it took us into shooting wars and now it's taken us into Iraq. Oh we've got a special relationship alright…'

Unable to bear looking at him as he spoke, I glanced across the room. On the mantelpiece the picture of his grandson in his smart uniform still smiled proudly out.

'And what has it got us? There's been a cost. A very real cost.'

Only now it was bordered by a black ribbon.

'And you, your family, have paid the price?' I asked. I didn't need to hear his reply.

And at last I understood.

For all the talk of principles. For all his rationalisation about Britain's place in the world, the loss of the empire, our subservient role. In the end none of it had been enough to make him act. It all came down to the personal, it always did.

A dead brother, lost in a useless mission without the equipment he needed to make a success of it.

A dead father, sacrificed in a last unacknowledged desperate gamble for king and country.

And now a dead grandson, lost in a useless mission without the equipment he needed to make a success of it either.

And an old man's anger was about to change the history books and the world's relations forever.

Chapter 13

Aircraft and the U-Boat have turned surface fleets into obsolete playthings.

Adolf Hitler, 1934

I glanced down at the printed words laid out on the lectern in front of me. I'd practised it so many times over the last couple of days I felt like I knew it off by heart, but as I looked back and out at the sea of faces it was comforting to know they were there. Mum was in the front row, surrounded by the grandchildren and comforted by my sisters in law. My brothers were in the row behind. Familiar faces to fix onto as I began to speak.

'Hello everyone,' I began.

'I'm here as a son, and on behalf of our whole family, to thank you all for coming, and to talk to you about my father,' and I read out his whole name, the one nobody knew him by.

'Except I'm not.

'Today we are all here to remember Dad,' and I said the familiar name everybody used every day, 'the man we all knew, and where do you start?

'Well really it ought to be with a cup of tea, because as far as Dad was concerned, the first thing that should happen whenever anyone came to visit was to offer tea and something to eat all round.

'In fact, *Polly Put the Kettle On* was one suggestion for the first bit of music we should hear today, however that got overruled as Dad was a man who you will all come to realise over the next half an hour, if you didn't already know, was a fan of both Country *and* Western, as the old joke has it.

'But when we were wondering how to start this talk properly, one of the condolence calls to Mum really did the job for us as it summed up everything we need to say today, when Dad was described as, 'An exceptionally kind and generous man, with a gentle nature and a wicked sense of humour.'

'That's Dad to a T.

'Now, there's a saying about young looking policemen but, in this case, it was true. Sixty years ago, it was a very sick nineteen-year-old, newly minted constable, down with the flu, when his landlady asked a fellow lodger, a young teacher, to help nurse him, and the rest as they say is history.

'Dad had joined the RUC on leaving school after his A levels out of a need to help support his family, and always said he left when they wanted to issue him with a gun. This in a town where the height of IRA activity until then had been to blow up the local scout hut.

'Mum and Dad moved to England, getting married with the grand sum of £100 to their name and promptly went off that afternoon to buy a set of cutlery and crockery for two.'

*

I went with the public, authorised, version. This wasn't the time or the place for the truth. You never knew who did or didn't know it.

'Dad came sixth nationally in the Civil Service exam to become a Customs Officer first at London Docks and then at Heathrow, until his ill health forced his early retirement, in which he pursued his hobbies.

'As a youngster, due to family problems Dad spent some very formative years in the heart of the Irish countryside, which left him with a lifelong interest in gardening and growing things, and an abiding love of peace, sunshine and putting home grown fruit on the table.

'And of course, having grown a very impressive vine amongst it all, the practical man in him couldn't help but start to ferment his own wine, as grandchildren who were pressed into treading the grapes in a washing up bowl remember vividly.

'Those coming back to join us afterwards will be pleased to know that his home-made rocket-fuel probably isn't behind the bar, although given the gallons that this essentially teetotal man made there may still be some lurking somewhere.

'The same period also gave him a lifelong and quite lucrative interest in horse racing, which with his subscription to the *Racing Post* he bet on very successfully using a system which sadly none of the rest of us were ever able to fully grasp.

'And of course, he always had an equally sporting and acutely intelligent interest in politics.

'As children, I guess my brothers and I just assumed everyone's Dad wrote comprehensive and erudite notes on their daily copy of *The Guardian* explaining what was really going on behind the stories, before regularly tearing out articles to stick up on the kitchen noticeboard, or post off to whoever in the family might be interested.

'So retirement gave him the opportunity to fulfil a lifetime's dream by taking a degree in History and Politics, even if it did mean lodging as an undergraduate in my house in Reading while he did so. (Of course there were strict rules, No drugs! No loud parties, Dad!)'

*

'Everyone who ever met Dad will remember his enduring characteristics.

'Dad was honest and unpretentious. He would happily answer the door wearing a 'hand-me-up' Iron Maiden tour T-shirt he was pottering around the house in.

'Perhaps it was his Civil Service background, or more likely it was just him, but he was always very, very organised, and could be serious about some things.

'He was Mr Lists, and once something was on his shopping list, it got bought every week, whether it was needed or not, oh and woe betide the junior managers in Waitrose when they moved something on their shelves, as they'd find themselves being buttonholed and asked, *Where are you hiding the jam* (or whatever it might be) *this week?*

'And he was Mr Routine. You could set your watch by his dinner time, and while grandchildren always found it miraculous the way the breakfast table was magically set each morning, it was of course because granddad always did it the night before, probably after having checked the weather on Ceefax of which he was the last known user, and had a last digestive biscuit, something he was never knowingly more than ten feet away from at any time.

'But over and above these traits, he was Mr Kind, Caring and Generous. Dad was a man who would do anything for anybody.'

*

'Family always came first, he always said, usually as he stuffed cash or sweets into a young person's pocket at the end of a visit.

'And as family, my brothers and I knew, Dad, and Mum, were always there for us, for whatever we needed, supporting us to be successful and become what we wanted to be. And in many ways, for us, I think that's going to be our best tribute to him.

'But in truth whether you were a neighbour, a friend, a child or grandchild's friend, or even a greedy squirrel in the garden, it didn't matter, he was kind to everyone, and almost everyone he met became family to some degree.

'The number of neighbours and friends here today is testament to that.

'And everything he did, it was always with a very dry sense of humour which never took anyone too seriously, particularly himself.

'As his grandchildren recall, he might always feed the dogs under the table – but he was always ready to brazenly deny it with a grin on his face if challenged.'

*

'Of course, Dad wasn't perfect. All information was always treated as being on a strictly need to know basis. He was colour blind for example, a fact I for one wasn't aware of at all until he took me out for my first driving lesson, and told me to pull out onto the main road *After the green car...* To which the only meaningful response was, *What green car?*

'So let's remember Dad, an exceptionally kind and generous man, with a gentle nature and a wicked sense of humour, and when you do, please remember the last time he made you laugh.

'And please remember someone who will be sorely missed, by his family, by his friends, and by some very fat, muesli loving, squirrels.'

I sat down as my brothers and their children stood up and made their way to the podium to read out the poems they had picked.

> *If you can keep your head when all about you*
> *Are losing theirs and blaming it on you,*
> *If you can trust yourself when all men doubt you,*
> *But make allowance for their doubting too;*
> *If you can wait and not be tired by waiting,*
> *Or being lied about, don't deal in lies...*

*

'What the hell are you doing here?' I demanded as I strode up to where Sir Tom was standing just off to one side of the main body of mourners gathered on the grass in the garden of remembrance just outside the exit.

'Congratulations, good speech,' he said.

'Thank you,' I told him, in a tone which made it plain I was waiting for an answer.

'I'm just here to pay my respects. As an old colleague as it were,' he met my glower, and then cast his eyes over the crowd inviting me to join him. 'Think I'm the only one here from the Services other than your friend there?' he said nodding towards where Libby was standing by the door, elegant as ever in a dark suit. 'In an official or unofficial capacity. Think again.'

But I wasn't interested in anyone else he might want to point out just at that moment. I just wanted an answer from him. 'Just leave her out of it will you? And answer me this if you want to talk. So why did you do it? You and my Dad?'

'I had my reasons, he had his,' he said.

'Which were?'

'He wanted you to get your big break.'

I took a moment to digest this.

'Don't you want him to have died for something?' he challenged me, before adding, 'Especially given the circumstances...'

I just looked at him. Willing him to confirm my suspicions/

'You know what I'm talking about. No clues at the burglary? Nothing taken? Who the hell do you think was responsible for your father's death?'

'You mean...'

'I'm sorry, we never meant for this to happen when we first discussed it, your father and I, but looking back we should have anticipated it. They were always keeping tabs on you, still are from what I can see,' he said his eyes flicking across to Libby again as she watched our conversation. I didn't like what he was implying.

'Once you started digging, the Service was bound to notice sooner or later and, not just the Service. Then they and the cousins were going to go looking for your source...'

'The cousins?'

'Yes, and they're not too subtle at times. A bit cowboy in fact...'

'And of course, they'd take a look at Dad, is that what you are telling me?' I demanded.

He shrugged, 'Well he'd be a natural starting point, wouldn't he? Someone they'd want to have a good look at, a very close look at indeed, if you understand what I'm saying.'

I understood him perfectly.

'I see...' I told him. But of course, whatever I thought, and whether he was right or not, it didn't make a blind bit of difference.

We'd already had this argument, back in his study. There was no way that I was going to get the BBC to broadcast what he wanted. In fact, if anything, the lengths he'd just suggested the secret services would go to in order to keep this secret made it even less likely.

In the UK.

'So, will you help?' he asked.

I looked over at Mum and then back at him.

But then there was a precedent, I thought.

'You'd be arrested,' I told him, 'if you stay, you're risking jail.'

'I've made my decision,' he told me calmly, 'I'll stand by it and take my chances.'

We stood facing each other for a moment.

'Have you made yours?' he asked.

'I've got to get back,' I said, sticking out my hand, 'but I will think about it.'

*

If the BBC and British institutions were no good for putting something out, then there were always other ways. Ones we knew had worked in the past.

Looking me straight in the eye, he shook my hand without saying anything, and then abruptly he wheeled around and was quickly lost in the crowd.

While without looking at it or giving any sign, I slipped the memory stick he'd palmed into my hand into my pocket while I slowly looked around the knots of people talking on the grass. Some of them I knew; family, friends, neighbours new and old. But then there were many, many I didn't who could have been anybody from any time in Mum and Dad's life together dating back to before I was born, or could have been anybody at all. And without quizzing Mum directly, there was no way I was ever going to know.

If I had a manuscript, then there was the *Spycatcher* option for example, arranging for publication in Australia beyond the effective remit of the UK authorities. Perhaps backed up by posting the evidence online, his videoed statement on YouTube for example. If you put enough material out there on enough forums and in enough forms, in reality there was going to be little the authorities could do once the genie was out of the bottle.

And in the few steps it took to return to be beside where Mum was speaking to one of the well-wishers, I had made up my mind.

I'd have to distance myself from Libby. That would be hard but it wouldn't be fair otherwise, she had a career of her own to think about.

But fuck it, yes. I would do it.

For Dad.

Background, bibliography and notes

I think I see my way through.

Do you mean that we can avoid defeat?

Of course, I mean we can beat them, I shall drag the United States in.

Conversation with his father on 18 May 1940,
reported by Randolph Churchill

This book is a work of fiction set against the background of historical events and public figures such as Churchill and Eden.

The story described and the characters portrayed are however fictional and any resemblance to actual persons, living or dead, is purely coincidental. Obviously, the fictional Press Commission in this book has no relation to the actual Press Commission.

As stated at the outset, this novel is a work of fiction, but it is one based on facts, and for anyone interested in the real documents and events underlying this narrative the following sources may be of interest.

For convenience, live links to the key sites and books referred to below can be found on my website at http://www.bad-press.co.uk/sources.html

*

The dictum *Countries don't have friends, only interests*, has been widely used by politicians and goes back in various forms to Lord Palmerston, and has always seemed very relevant to the reality of the US and UK's relationship both during, and since, the Second World War.

The genesis of this book was coming across the strange story of the *SS Automedon* and the incredible loss of its top-secret cargo, an unmitigated intelligence disaster from any point of view.

Both Captain Bernhard Rogge (*Under Ten Flags*) and his ADC Ulrich Mohr (*Atlantis*) wrote accounts of the *Atlantis*'s two-year cruise during which she sank twenty-one ships and twice the tonnage the allies lost to the much more famous pocket cruiser *Graf Spee*.

The Cabinet Office memo to CinC Far East, Air Chief Marshall Sir Robert

Brooke-Popham detailing the fundamental weakness of the British position and our likely inability to successfully counter Japanese aggression in the theatre is a real document. It is also the case that when Brooke-Popham asked about its whereabouts after the war he was given the 'lost to U-boat action' story.

In fact, information about its capture in transit on the SS *Automedon* by the *Atlantis* (see https://en.wikipedia.org/wiki/SS_Automedon) was only exposed when the American wartime decrypts of Japanese intelligence reports were released in 1980. They were certainly not revealed by anything released by Britain, for which it would appear this was still too embarrassing a revelation some forty-five years after the end of the war (see the CIA record https://www.cia.gov/library/readingroom/docs/CIA-RDP90-00965R000605710002-4.pdf).

And I do find it odd that a memo of that importance which was written on 8 August 1940 and intended for the CinC Far East was still en route when it was captured on 11 November 1940, almost 3 months later… coincidentally the same date as the Royal Navy's aerial torpedo attack on the Italian fleet in Taranto harbour.

In terms of America's stance in the Pacific in 1940 and attitude towards Japanese aggression the McCollum memorandum is available online as both a scanned copy and text (which has some typos) at http://www.whatreallyhappened.com/WRHARTICLES/McCollum/index.html.

Swordfish by David Wragg gives the story of the Taranto raid, while Walter Lord's *Day of Infamy* is the classic history of Pearl Harbour.

Again, it is a matter of record that the Japanese assistant naval attaché in Berlin, Lt Cdr Takeshi Naito, travelled to Taranto to investigate the British attack on the Italian fleet on the night of 11 November 1940 (followed by a high-powered delegation the following year). On his return to Japan he then passed on his findings to Cmdr Mitsuo Fuchida who went on to lead the attack on Pearl Harbour just over a year later on 7 December 1941.

The potential lessons to be learnt from the British attack at Taranto were the subject of exchanges of memos within the US navy. The use of anti-torpedo baffles for protection against torpedo plane attacks within harbours were for example Exhibits 17 and 19 in the Hart Enquiry and are online at https://www.ibiblio.org/pha/timeline/410215acno.html and https://www.ibiblio.org/pha/timeline/410613acno.html.

The figures on British bombing accuracy come from the Butt report of 1941 https://en.wikipedia.org/wiki/Butt_Report.

And sadly the photograph of the *USS Arizona* in the November 1941 Army-Navy game and its caption is only too real https://collectableivy.wordpress.com/2009/02/22/army-navy-program-1941-uss-arizona.

Those interested in further detail about some of the subjects covered in general might like to read *Hitler's Armada* by Geoff Hewitt, *Japan's Blitzkreig* by Bernard Edwards, *Deception in World War II* by Charles Cruikshank, *Churchill's Wizards* by Nicholas Rankin, *The Code Book* by Simon Singh, *Defence of the Realm*, the authorised history of MI5 by Christopher Andrew, *Enigma* by Hugh Sebag-Montefiore, or *Military Intelligence Blunders* by Colonel John Hughes-Wilson, and of course spend hours surfing Wikipedia which is a truly wonderful research tool and distraction for writers.

The excerpts from the translation of Hitler's Directive 16 are from *Silent Victory* by Duncan Grinnell-Milne as quoted by Geoff Hewitt in *Hitler's Armada*.

None of the views expressed are those of the author.

Or necessarily of my father...

Thanks and a couple of requests

Dear Reader

I want to take this opportunity to say thank you for reading *Best of Enemies.* I hope you enjoyed reading it and I have two requests.

Firstly, I'd love your feedback.

So please do leave a review on Amazon, whether you loved it or hated it, just let me know.

Reader reviews are the lifeblood of any writer's career, they help tell us what's working so we can give you more of it, and what isn't so we can change it; and they're also vitally important for getting our books noticed whether it's by readers browsing online or by being able to submit books on advertising services, so every review means a lot to me.

Secondly, I'd like your help to spread the word.

Word of mouth recommendations are without doubt the most powerful force in helping a book to succeed so if you've enjoyed this book, please tell your friends about it both in person and via social media.

Finally, I'd also like to take the opportunity to give something back for your help, so, if you're not already part of my readers' group please do head over to my website at www.bad-press.co.uk and join in by requesting the free short story e-book offer for your copy of *How To Win The Lottery*.

Thanks again.

Iain

About the author

Iain Parke imports industrial quantities of Class A drugs, kills people and lies (a lot) for a living, being a British based crime fiction writer.

Armed with an MBA degree, he worked in insolvency and business restructuring in the UK and Africa which inspired his first novel *The Liquidator*, a conspiracy thriller set in East Africa. Whatever you do, don't take it on holiday as your safari reading!

This was then followed by his 'Biker Lit' crime thriller *Heavy Duty People*, set amongst UK outlaw bikers in the North East and Borders; which turned first into a trilogy, now optioned for TV, and then into a longer series.

Today Iain lives off the grid, high up on the North Pennines in Northumberland with his wife, dogs, and a garage full of motorcycle restoration projects where he's always working on a number of projects.

For more about Iain's work please visit www.bad-press.co.uk and/or connect with Iain on social media:

iainparke@hotmail.com
Facebook: /Iain.Parke
Goodreads: /author/show/4400967.Iain_Parke
Pinterest: /iainparke
LinkedIn: /iainparke
Twitter: @iainparke

The Liquidator

Dangerous things happen in Africa. People disappear. Everybody knows that.

But as an outsider, Paul thinks he is safe, even from the secret police, whatever he starts to find, or wherever it leads; despite the turmoil leading up to the country's first multi-party election and with a diamond fuelled civil war raging in the failed state just across the border.

But when Paul finds himself and his friends trapped holding a potentially deadly secret as the country begins to implode, what will he be prepared to do to protect himself and those around him in order to escape?

Set in East Africa in the wake of the Rwandan genocide, civil war in Burundi and the first stirrings of Islamic terrorism in the region, this contemporary political thriller draws on both recent events and the historical legacies of slavery to paint a dark picture of potentially shocking danger to the West.

Heavy Duty People

"A fantastic anti-hero - positively Shakespearian in his moral complexity - If I could only recommend one book this year, it would be *Heavy Duty People*" Vulpes Libris

Your club and your brothers are your life - Damage

Damage's club has had an offer it can't refuse, to patch over to join The Brethren.

But what does this mean for Damage and his brothers?

What choices will they have to make? What history might it reawaken? And why is The Brethren making this offer?

Loyalty to his club and his brothers has been Damage's life and route to wealth, but what happens when business becomes serious and brother starts killing brother?

When being in a gang turns into being a gangster, Sons of Anarchy meets Get Carter in this gritty UK set biker noir crime thriller.

Now in development as a TV series

THE ACCLAIMED SAGA CONTINUES

Leaving Cedar Ridge Farm, Gregory had to travel along a state road for a while. He saw the usual assortment of Amish buggies with their red brake lights and the caution triangle glued to the back....

He had to admit, the Amish were firm in their determination not to be seduced by the conveniences of the world, committed to staying separate and distinct. Keeping apart was the glue that kept them together....

Sometimes he even wondered what it would be like to "become Amish." He had no idea if that were even possible.

But whenever he thought of Rebecca, he found himself hoping that it was.

> — From *Fork in the Crick*

***

"Rebecca Zook, 22, a talented quilt maker in the Amish community of Lancaster County, Pennsylvania, is getting past the point of getting married and starting a family[.] Burgess makes good use of his setting. Rebecca's Amish culture isn't just a backdrop; it's part of her. Her quilts rework images from her family's daily life, such as the saddles and leather goods made by her father, while still honoring tradition. The gentle love story also respects Rebecca's values. **A sensitive story about finding oneself in a community.**"

> — *Kirkus Reviews* (on *Stone in the Crick*, Book 1 of
> *Rebecca Zook's Amish Romance*)